Lavender Blue

"Billy, don't go yet!" Lily cried "_____ o sign a contract if you're gettin_____ ny, I'm hungry. Come f_____

Billy gave _____ take crumbs from _____ his voice.

"Be like that, t_____ nd anger burning inside her. Ho_____ er like that when she was truly only tryin_____ friends like they used to be?

Yet still she felt obliged to try one final time. "What's wrong, Billy? Why don't you want to know me any more?" she implored him, her voice breaking as she spoke. She missed him so much. He had been such a big part of her life. They had shared so much fun, so much music, all their hopes and dreams...

Also available in the Forget Me Not series:

Forget me Not

Lavender Blue

Lorna Read

SCHOLASTIC

Scholastic Children's Books
Commonwealth House,
1–19 New Oxford Street,
London WC1A 1NU, UK
A division of Scholastic Ltd
London ~ New York ~ Toronto ~ Sydney ~ Auckland

First published by Scholastic Ltd, 1998

Copyright © Lorna Read, 1998

ISBN 0 590 13940 1

Typeset by TW Typesetting, Midsomer Norton Somerset

Made and printed by Cox & Wyman Ltd., Reading, Berks

10 9 8 7 6 5 4 3 2 1

Chapter 1

The singing came from a top-floor window of a tall, narrow house. The woman's voice sounded like melted butter poured over little, tender new potatoes. Like honey on hot bread. Like the warm coconut smell of gorse blossom in the spring.

Though sometimes it was more like frost on a silver bell, like lemon icing, tinglingly tart before the sweetness set in. James Graydon was not a poet but these sorts of thoughts came to him whenever he heard that voice, and he blessed the day he had cut down Betterton Street to Drury Lane, instead of taking his normal route down Long Acre.

One day, he promised himself, he would find the owner of that voice. It was his business to.

It was the worst day of Lily Cobbett's life. As she trudged home in the rain from Chancery Lane to Covent Garden, it was difficult to tell which were raindrops on her cheeks and which were tears.

"Oi, girl, watch where you're going. I nearly 'ad you then!" bawled the driver of a delivery cart, reining his horse so hard to the left to avoid colliding with Lily that the animal neighed as the bit jarred in its mouth.

Lily's response was to shake her head dully, sending her

wet strands of black hair flicking out in a spray of rain-water. Mud and horse droppings mired her shoes. Her stockings were soaked through and filthy, and the hem of her dark grey skirt was sodden and black as she crossed High Holborn in a daze and slipped into Little Turnstile, one of the gloomy alleys which led through to Lincoln's Inn Fields.

It was twenty past three on a Thursday afternoon in November, 1898, and already it was growing dark. Ahead of her, a lamplighter was touching his pole to a streetlamp. The gas light flickered green, then settled down to a yellow glow, illuminating the flicking tail of a rat as it scuttled to a darker, more secret hiding-place.

Lily shuddered. She hated rats. Some men made their living by catching them and selling them to public houses where the chief form of entertainment provided was rat-killing contests. Men would bring their terriers and chuck them into a pit of rats, and put down bets as the slaughter took place. Ugh! How could men do such things? wondered Lily. Once, when her father had been out of work, he had considered becoming a rat catcher. Only the outcries and pleadings of herself and her older sisters had made him think twice about it. Her brothers had thought it was a jolly good idea.

It was quieter here in the back streets away from the hubbub of Kingsway. Quieter, but more dangerous. Her mother had warned her not to walk through Lincoln's Inn Fields alone as it was a haunt of pickpockets, drunkards and many other types of villain. But Lily considered herself wise to the ways of the street. She had known this area of London all her life. From the slums of Clerkenwell, where her grandfather still lived, to the overcrowded, crime-ridden courts of Seven Dials where her mother had been born, sixteen-year-old Lily knew every twist and turning, every shop and alley. When you lived in two rooms with your parents and six brothers and sisters, it was very necessary to spend a lot of time outdoors.

It was better now that four had left home. Her oldest brother, Edward, had joined the Navy and two of her older sisters, Millie and Edie, were married.

Elizabeth, whose eyesight had always been poor, had gone to work as a governess for a rich family in Shropshire. She had a flair for languages and had studied hard at French and Italian. Her schoolteachers had been so pleased with her that they had given her extra lessons free, knowledge which she was now attempting to pass on to her two young, spoilt charges, Master Samuel and Mistress Clarissa Ingsby of Monkstanton Grange, Shawbury. Just how she managed to correct their exercise books, Lily couldn't possibly imagine. They had all clubbed together to buy her a powerful magnifying glass to supplement her spectacles, before she left to take up her post.

Lily sighed as she plodded home by the circuitous route she had chosen. She was the only one who had failed her mother, Cecily. Everybody else was doing well. Cecily's own mother had come from quite a posh family who had lived in St Albans. If only she had stayed there, and not met Kenneth, Lily's grandfather, their lives might have been totally different. But marriage to him had dragged her down – down all the way to the noisy, teeming Seven Dials, where Lily's mother had been born. It was hearing her own mother's stories of how much better life could be, and how education mattered, even for girls, that had given Cecily so much ambition for her own children. She was determined to see all the girls marry well, and thought it important that all of them should have a skill to fall back on, should husbands fail them. Cecily was a first-class seamstress and dressmaker. Her skill with a needle had earned her steady pennies over the years – pennies which Lily's father, Charlie, seemed determined to drink away. Any man could turn into a drunkard, according to Cecily: marriage was a gamble and the longer you waited before tying the knot, the more experienced you would be in reading the signs and have a chance to sever the engagement before things had gone too far.

Her mother would not be expecting her before seven at the earliest as Mr Collyer never closed his drapery shop before six-thirty. Lily missed her nineteen-year-old sister greatly. She and Elizabeth had always lain next to each other in the bed they shared with Millie. Edie, being very fat, had had her own mattress on the floor in the corner.

Edward and Harry had slept in the room intended as the living-room, while her parents and any child who was sick slept in the kitchen by the warmth of the kitchen stove. But now Father and Harry, who was only sixteen months older than Lily, had the living-room to themselves while Lily had to sleep with her mother and baby Archibald, so named because he was born without a single hair on his head. And these days the kitchen range was often cold.

They would be able to afford even less coal for it now, Lily thought guiltily. What would Elizabeth say if she knew that Lily had been sacked from her very first job, the job her sister Millie had worked so hard to get for her? How on earth was she going to deliver the news to her mother, who was banking on her income in order to pay the rent arrears?

Lily's father, Charlie, was a good-natured fellow who worked as a porter in Covent Garden market and had introduced Harry to the portering trade. He was an excellent musician and he and his tin whistle were known at alehouses from Smithfield to the Strand. What a shame he never thought of making any money from it, thought Lily. He could whistle up such a cheery jig that crowds of singing, stamping men would line up the drinks for him and once he was in his cups, he would buy a round for everyone in the pub and return home with empty pockets.

Lily's mother despaired of the man she had married, yet she must still love him, thought Lily. Why else would she have had baby Archibald? Despite the fact that the rent was so often not paid, Lily heard them laughing together more often than they argued. Charlie was such a sunny personality, with his red hair and Irish charm, that it was impossible not to like him. Lily loved him, particularly as he alone, of all the family, appreciated and encouraged her own musical talent. Oh, the nights they had had in her childhood, when everyone was at home! Father on the whistle, Lily singing, Edward banging a saucepan for a drum, Harry on comb and paper... They would dance and make music until the neighbours banged on the walls, or else begged to be allowed to join in.

But those days were finished now and it was all Archibald's fault, thought Lily resentfully. If only Mother hadn't had him! He was a fretful, whining, smelly baby and

Mother had been sick ever since his birth. And, with such an enormous gap between him and Lily, there was no way he would ever be able to enjoy the closeness the rest of his siblings had had. Archie was a small, ugly, scrawny cuckoo in the nest and Lily often wished they could tip him out when he screamed and bawled in the night and ruined her slumber.

A warm, earthy smell scented the air. Lily sniffed and her stomach contracted and rumbled with hunger. It was a baked-potato man, with his iron potato baker and the spikes on which newly baked potatoes were placed to await their purchasers.

Lily felt in her pocket. Although he had been very cross with her, Mr Collyer had at least had the decency to pay up the amount he owed her for the four days she had worked that week. She knew she should bring every penny of that two shillings and threepence back to her mother, but ... oh, she was *so* hungry and she knew what supper would be. A bit of cat's fish, boiled with a half-rotten turnip or some cabbage leaves Harry had filched from beneath a stall in the market.

Her stomach curdled at the thought – and she felt even sicker thinking of how the flat would smell, a mixture of cheap fish, boiled cabbage and the pungent stink of Archie's napkins, rows of which were forever drying on a piece of string in front of the kitchen range.

She asked for a potato and handed over her pennies. "Wotcher, darlin'! Here's a nice fresh one. Put some roses in them cheeks," said the baked-potato man, handing Lily a red-hot potato wrapped in a piece of newspaper to prevent her from burning her hands.

Lily gazed at him with large eyes grey as London fog – eyes which were fringed with the long, dark lashes which were the envy of every female in her family.

("I can't think where you got those from," her mother had once said dubiously, "although my mother told me that her Aunt Clara was a great beauty of her day. She was said to have 'eyes like fern-fringed pools'.")

Now the baked-potato man was getting the benefit of those foggy, fern-fringed eyes and it was either the power of their unconscious beauty, or the pallor of her rain-lashed cheeks, which prompted him to hand her another screw of paper with a pat of butter in it. " 'Ere you are, stick this in your spud," he ordered her.

Lily thanked him, split her potato, dripped the melting butter into its powdery depths and delicately bit off a chunk. It was delicious. She swallowed and felt it warming her cold body all the way down.

She had planned to walk around for two hours before coming home, so as not to arouse her mother's suspicion, and then to leave for work at the normal time next morning and spend a day wandering, thus postponing the evil moment of telling the truth about her sacking for another day. But it was so cold and she was so wet that she knew if she walked round for much longer, she would catch her death. There was nothing for it. She would just have to go home and face the music.

Chapter 2

Lily crossed Kingsway and walked up Great Queen Street, then turned right into Drury Lane. The moment she turned the corner into Betterton Street, she could hear Archie's wails. Her baby brother had a particularly annoying squeal, rather like a wet finger run slowly down a window pane. It got to you and set your teeth right on edge.

Oh no, Lily thought. If Archie was fractious, that meant her mother would be in a bad mood – and if Mother was already in a bad mood, Lily's news would cause her to explode! Cecily had always had a hot temper, though she normally cooled down quickly and apologized.

Outside the house Lily dithered and shivered, getting wetter and wetter. Her delay was ended by a great sneeze which exploded from her, racking her slender body and sending another fine spray of rainwater flicking from her dripping hair.

"Goodness gracious child, you're soaked through!"

Just at the moment when Lily's hand was hovering on the doorhandle, it was flung open and great, fat, red-faced Mrs Molloy who owned the house and lived on the ground floor came out. It was Mrs Molloy's copious kitchen which supplied the water for the rest of the household. It must have been a constant inconvenience for her, having the other tenants forever tripping down the stairs with a variety of receptacles in order to take water back up to their rooms, but she always remained good-humoured and, now that her own brood of nine children had flown, acted as a general mother to the rest of the occupants.

The only toilet the house possessed was the earth closet in Mrs Molloy's back yard. Mrs Molloy's system of humorous notices saying whether it was occupied or not, and at what time it could be expected to be free, cheered up the waiting time. Chamber pots were in use throughout the house, as one lavatory could hardly service the needs of Mrs Molloy's family and all the tenants.

It would take more than Mrs Molloy's sense of humour to cheer Lily up right now, though. "I'm quite all right," she mumbled, and made to dodge past the portly woman, but Mrs Molloy caught her arm.

"Come into the kitchen and take a cup of tea with a lonely old woman," she insisted. "The old man's out. He's visiting his friend Tom, the one who has the pigeons. He won't be back for hours."

Mrs Molloy fussed over the wet girl, making her take off her dripping clothes and hanging them to steam in front of her roaring fire, then giving her a peat-coloured woollen shawl to wrap around herself and a big towel with which to dry her hair.

While Lily was blotting her face and wringing out her hair, Mrs Molloy busied herself with the heavy black iron kettle on the range. She made the tea in a big brown earthenware teapot and left it to draw while she lifted two currant buns from the griddle on which they were cooling.

"I made these this afternoon," she said. "Give me your

honest opinion, colleen. Have I put in too much baking soda?"

Lily reached for the plate of buns and bit into one. Despite the baked potato, she still felt hungry. The bun did have a slightly odd flavour, but it was still delicious. "I think it's fine," she told her neighbour.

Mrs Molloy poured the tea into two large mugs. "You don't mind not having the best china?" she asked Lily, who shook her head. "I prefer these, you get more in them," confided the jolly woman, laughing so that her chins wobbled.

She waited in silence until Lily had gulped down some of the scalding tea. Archie's wailing could be heard faintly, drifting down the stairwell.

"He's got a good pair of lungs on him, that he has," remarked Mrs Molloy.

Lily nodded.

"It must be hard for your mother, not being in the best of health. It happens sometimes, with afterthoughts," Mrs Molloy continued.

Lily frowned. What were 'afterthoughts'? Then she realized that the woman was talking about babies which weren't intended, and happened as accidents after the rest of the family were grown up.

Mrs Molloy ploughed relentlessly on, as if determined to get to the bottom of some mystery. "I suppose she needs you more than ever now," she said.

Lily felt a lump of tears rise into her throat.

Mrs Molloy leaned forward as far as her bulk would allow her, and laid a red, work-worn hand on Lily's knee. "Is that why you're looking like a month of wet Sundays?"

she enquired. Then, when Lily didn't reply, she went on, "You're back very early tonight, aren't you? Mr Collyer closed his shop?"

Staring into her cup of tea and trying to hold back the tears, Lily confided in a small voice, "I … I haven't got a job there any more. Mr Collyer said I was inattentive. I was…"

"Singing, I suppose," supplied Mrs Molloy.

"Yes. It was a really boring afternoon with no customers, so I left the front of the shop and went into the back and looked out of the window. There's a tree growing in the yard, a beautiful ash tree, and I started singing, 'The oak and the ash and the –'"

"'– bonny ivy tree,'" Mrs Molloy chimed in. "I know the one. What then?"

"Well, two customers had come in and I didn't hear them because I was singing. But they must have called out and rung the bell and Mr Collyer was in his office upstairs and he came down and…" She turned her huge, expressive eyes to Mrs Molloy and shrugged.

"And now you haven't got a job any more. Well, it's not the end of the world. A pretty, talented girl like you. Your father works at the market – so does Harry. Can't they find you some work there?"

Lily bit her lip, wondering how to tell her neighbour that Mrs Cobbett had better things planned for her youngest daughter than working amongst the coarse market women. The market was all right for men, especially if, like Harry, they didn't have the brains to do anything else, but was no place for a woman, in Cecily's opinion. She wanted Lily to have a genteel job like Elizabeth. The drapery store had been perfect.

"I'll ask them," she promised Mrs Molloy. Then, setting down her empty mug, she rose to her feet.

Mrs Molloy rose with her. "Take these to your mother. There's one each for her, your father and Harry." She handed Lily three buns.

"What about Archie?" Lily asked cheekily.

Mrs Molloy's small, black, curranty eyes twinkled and she handed Lily another bun, knowing who it was really for.

There was no way anyone could climb the wooden stairs without being heard. Every one echoed and creaked.

"Is that you, Charlie?" she heard her mother call.

"No, it's not, it's me," Lily replied, turning her key in the lock.

"*WAAAAAAH!*" came from Archie.

"Shut up!" Lily shouted fiercely.

"Don't you speak to your little brother like that. Babies can't help it," her mother snapped back.

She was looking ... well, worn out was an understatement, thought Lily. Her mother looked shocking – pale to the point of deathly, her black hair thin and streaked with grey, her eyes sunken hollows. She went to speak to her daughter then coughed and clutched her chest.

"Are you ill, Mother?" Lily asked anxiously.

"Just tired," her mother replied, rocking the wicker cradle in which Archie lay. "I had six children who were all good babies, but this one never sleeps."

Lily knew that only too well. "Mrs Molloy gave me these to give you," she said. She handed them all over without taking the extra one intended for herself. Her mother deserved to have two.

"Is that her shawl you're wearing?" her mother asked.

"Yes. She saw how wet I was when I came in and she's got my clothes down there, drying."

"Do you think she'd like a few nappies to dry as well?"

It was the first time in ages that Lily had heard her mother attempt a joke and she laughed encouragingly. Then she wondered why her mother hadn't asked why she was home early.

"Could you go out to the butcher's for me? Get two penn'orth of mince?" her mother requested.

"Of course. I've got some money," Lily offered and was off down the stairs before the subject of conversation was changed. It wasn't until she got out of the house that she realized that she was wearing nothing but Mrs Molloy's shawl above her petticoat! Fortunately, the woollen garment was as voluminous as its owner and Lily excited no rude comments as she darted between the slanting rain-drops to the butcher's in Drury Lane.

He was about to close and was just sweeping sawdust out on to the pavement as Lily panted out her errand. She knew why her mother had sent her now. If you went at closing time, the butcher was likely to be generous with any scraps he wanted to get rid of.

"And here's a bone for that dog of yours," he said, handing Lily a bloody parcel.

Lily was aware that the butcher knew that they didn't have a dog. She grinned and he winked back. "Thanks," she called, turning on her heel and darting back up Betterton Street. She knew her mother would be able to boil up the bone into nourishing soup and nobody needed that nourishment more than her mother, who was having a difficult time trying to feed Archie.

She noticed something different as soon as she got half-way up the stairs. Archie had stopped crying! She walked through the door with a smile on her lips, but the expression on her mother's face erased it.

"Mrs Molloy's brought your clothes up," she said.

That could only mean one thing – and her worst fear was confirmed by her mother saying, "How could you, Lily... How *could* you!"

"It wasn't my fault—" Lily began.

"Of course it was your fault, child," her mother replied sharply. "You were being inattentive. You're always inattentive, it's your worst fault and I should know, being your mother! You're a dreamer, Lily. You get that far-away look on your face and you don't hear what's spoken to you, you're miles away. Just like you are now!"

"What?" It was true. While her mother had been telling her off, Lily had drifted off to a place where she would far rather be – up on an imaginary stage, singing her heart out to an invisible audience.

"Oh, Lily!" her mother exclaimed in exasperation. Then she winced and put a hand to her head. "Oh dear, I think I'm getting one of my headaches."

"Can I get you anything?" Lily asked in a whisper. The headaches often led to dreadful bouts of sickness and she would do anything to prevent her poor mother having to endure one of those.

"No, dear, just sit down quietly." Cecily Cobbett sighed deeply. "Tell me exactly what happened, and then we'll try to think what you should do next."

Lily confessed, then said, "Mrs Molloy thinks I should get a job in the market, or as a flower seller."

"No daughter of mine is going to work in the market."
It was the response Lily had expected. "The market's quite
all right for your father, and for Harry, but you've got a
good brain in your head and I don't want you mixing with
those uneducated men and women. They'd drag you down
to their level, sure as anything. No, we must find you
something genteel. A milliner's, perhaps. They often need
pretty girls like you to model the hats."

Her mother smiled wanly. Her headache was obviously
paining her – but it had saved Lily from being shouted out
too badly. Now, seeing that familiar grey look on her
mother's face, Lily ached to cheer her up. A knitted tea-
cosy lay on the kitchen table. Lily seized it and popped it
on her head and was pleased when her mother burst out
laughing, despite her migraine. "Imagine you going to
Ascot with that on your head!" she said.

"And imagine *you* going to Ascot wearing this!" Lily
picked up the metal colander and placed it on her mother's
head. The handle hung over one ear at a rakish angle.
"Look!" she said, taking the mirror off the shelf and holding it up for her mother to see.

Their convulsions of laughter woke Archie. But instead
of crying this time, he started gurgling as if he, too, was
joining in the merriment.

When they had both finished wiping their eyes, Lily put
her arm round her mother's thin shoulders. "Don't worry,"
she said. "I'm sure I'll find something soon. I won't let you
starve."

"Huh! I wish your father thought the same way," her
mother snorted.

Lily glanced out of the window. "Oh look, it's stopped

raining," she observed. "I think I'll go and meet Harry."

"Well, I shall have a lie down while you're gone. It's not often that I get a bit of peace," Cecily Cobbett said. "You'll find the same when you get married and have children."

Lily grimaced. She had already decided that she would *never* marry and have children. Not if it meant being married to a ne'er-do-well husband whom you scarcely ever saw sober, and being squashed into two rooms with nappies all over the place, and having to walk up and down three flights of stairs to fetch a bucket of water. No, she would be like her Great-Aunt Clara, the beauty who had had many admirers but had never married. She would become a famous singer and have her own horses and carriage and a large house in a fashionable place like Mayfair.

Or maybe she could buy Windsor Castle or Hampton Court. Surely the Queen couldn't possibly live in them as well as in Buckingham Palace? It wasn't fair!

Lily put on an old dress, made by her mother, which she had almost grown out of. It was rather patched but was a cheerful ruby red. Wrapping Mrs Molloy's thick, warm shawl three times around herself and making a mental note to give it back to her as soon as she returned, she descended the creaky stairs and went out into the fresh, windy evening.

Soon the crowds would be mustering for that evening's entertainments at the nearby theatres, two of which, the Drury Lane Theatre and the Old Mo, were very close by indeed. The Old Mo's real name was the New Middlesex Music Hall, but all the locals called it the Old Mo because it was built on the site of the old Mogul Tavern, which had stood on that spot since the seventeen-hundreds.

If Lily had truly been going to the market to seek her brother, she would have turned left out of the front door, but instead she turned right, drawn by the sound of an accordion playing such a jolly tune that her feet started skipping in time to the music.

Outside the Old Mo, the fashionable crowds were already assembling and the street was a bustle of carriages and hansom cabs setting down their passengers. There was even a motor car or two, with gleaming brass lamps and funny wire wheels.

A tall, slender lad was leaning against the wall, a cloth cap at his feet, his hands working busily on the squeeze-box. His light tenor voice was singing one of the latest cheeky music-hall ditties. Lily's heart gave a little jump of excitement, as it always did when she saw him.

With his dark hair, vivid complexion, animated features and sparkling dark eyes, he resembled a gypsy, though there was no gypsy blood in Billy Morgan. He was Welsh through and through, born in the Valleys, the son of a coalminer. His father had been killed in an accident down the mine when Billy was nine years old and his mother had died soon afterwards – of grief, everybody said.

Relatives, overburdened with numerous children of their own and too poor to feed him, had wanted to lodge him with his stern grandmother, who didn't in the slightest want the responsibility of a lively little boy when she had fifteen grandchildren already by her various sons and daughters. Billy saved her the trouble of making room for him in her neat and tidy household by running away to London, taking his father's accordion with him.

He had avoided being put in an orphanage and sent to

school and had lived on his wits and his musical talent ever since. He was seventeen, eight months older than Lily, whose seventeenth birthday it would be in May. Lily had first encountered him four years ago when, like now, she had been drawn to him by his music.

"Billy!" Lily waved to him as she threaded her way between wheels and horses.

He looked at her and grinned, but his singing didn't falter, though his quick, warm smile made her heart miss a beat.

"Let me bottle for you," she said, picking up his cap. Collecting money for a busker was known as bottling even if you didn't actually use a bottle to collect the contributions in. With a fetching smile and a bobbing curtsey, Lily walked up and down the queues and quite a few gentlemen reached into their pockets and deposited a coin in the cap.

Now Billy's voice rose loud and clear in a minor key. He was singing about white rocks and a curlew keening on the moors over the bones of a lamb lying dead amongst the heather. The lamb was a symbol for the dead of old wars. It was a song which Billy had written himself and even though she had heard it many times, it always brought a tear to her eye. Now it was working its sad spell on the ladies in the crowd, who were reaching into their reticules and purses. Billy knew what he was doing all right, thought Lily as she bowed her head over the cap and received the money.

That song over, Billy started another. It was one everybody knew, made popular thirty years earlier by a famous music-hall artist called Harry Clifton. Lily knew it well.

Taking up a position at Billy's side, she joined in and sang harmony to his lead vocal.

"She was as beautiful as a butterfly, and as proud as a queen, Was pretty little Polly Perkins of Paddington Green…"

Chatter stopped and people looked their way, listening. Applause broke out when they finished, but Billy refused to acknowledge it and instead launched straight into another which he knew they could both sing, that old, haunting love song, *Greensleeves*. How Lily's voice soared. It reached the top note and hung there like a hovering lark, a note so pure that it thrilled the more sensitive members of their captive audience and made them shiver.

She knew she and Billy sang beautifully together. When they sang, she felt as if they had merged together and become one single musical instrument. It gave her a funny feeling, as if something was happening to her which she couldn't understand. She had never been kissed by a boy, but she often thought that it would join her to him and make her feel the way she felt when she sang with Billy. If only Billy *would* kiss her! He didn't seem to have a girl-friend and she certainly wasn't "walking out" with anyone. Her mother would have thought her far too young to have a sweetheart, even though some girls got married at sixteen or seventeen.

Cecily had married at eighteen and had her first child, Millie, at nineteen. "I don't want that to happen to you, Lily," she had often told her youngest daughter. "Falling in love is all very fine, but marriage is the end of a girl. You have no life after that. It's far better to wait, work a while, play the field, collect marriage proposals and choose the best of the bunch. That's what I should have done. Then I went and fell in love with your father, and look how that's turned out for us all!"

"But I don't want to be an old maid!" Lily had protested.

"You, my girl, will never be an old maid, I can assure you of that," her mother had said.

Lily wasn't so sure. What was "falling in love", anyway? Was it the bumpiness of her heart when she turned the corner of the street and saw Billy? Was it the melty feelings she got inside her when she heard him sing? Was it this wonderful sensation of being part of him when they sang, the feeling she had right now? Was it any of these things, or none at all?

When the song came to an end, Lily was aware of a strange silence. It was broken by the grinding sound of the theatre doors opening and a man's voice crying, "Everybody in, the performance will start in half an hour!"

Many coins were thrown their way. "Thank you, thank you," Lily said, scooping them into the hat.

Billy was fastening the straps round his accordion. Then he hefted it on to his shoulders. From a canvas bag strung around his wiry body, the handsome boy produced a scroll of paper and handed it to Lily. She unfolded it and saw that it was the words and music of a new song, one that was a current hit on the music halls.

"I know the tune," he said, "but can you teach me the words, Lily?"

Billy couldn't read or write, as he had never been to school, but he managed by getting other people to read aloud any letters that came to him. Lily had been taught to read by her mother, even before she started school. She longed to teach him the skill, but there was nowhere for them to go and be quiet together where they could rest paper and pencils and books, especially now that it was winter.

"Of course," Lily said. She would do anything for Billy. He was her very best friend – and also her deepest secret, for her family knew nothing of him. Her mother would have heartily disapproved of Lily consorting with a "street urchin". Lily knew that, even if she could persuade her mother to let him come visiting, the moment Mrs Cobbett realized that Billy was illiterate, she would do all she could to discourage their friendship, even if it meant locking Lily up in the house!

Billy gave her a shy smile. "We make a good team, you and I, don't you think?" he remarked.

The way he said it was rather odd, as if his words had some extra meaning which he expected Lily to understand.

"We do sing well together," she said, assuming that was what he had been referring to.

Billy seemed to sag a little. He moved away from her. Lily noticed a leaf caught in his thick curls and reached to pluck it out.

"Don't," he said, rather curtly.

"All right then, *be* like that," she said. He was just like her brothers. Moody. Maybe all boys were the same.

She started to read out the song words to him, then abruptly stopped as a blinding flash of inspiration hit her. Billy was making quite an acceptable living as a busker. And if *he* could do it, why couldn't she?

Chapter 3

Her mind spinning with the excitement of her new idea, Lily said goodbye to Billy, who was heading for the Theatre Royal, and set off to do what she had told her mother she would, which was find Harry before his father attempted to haul him off to a tavern and get him into "bad ways".

She knew exactly where she would find him. Harry was sweet on a girl called Dora who worked on a flower stall with her mother. When he wasn't wheeling stacks of cabbages on his barrow, he could be found flirting with Dora, who always wore a straw hat perched on top of her fair curls, whatever the time of year.

Sure enough, as Lily drew close to the stall which, with its masses of yellow and white chrysanthemums, looked like a patch of summer sunshine in the middle of winter, she spotted Harry. He saw her immediately, as his eyes were darting furtively around to make sure nobody was noticing him slacking.

"Hello, Sis!" he called.

"Good evening, Bro!" Lily called back. She loved Harry. He had a sunny nature like his father, and their relationship was strung together by a stream of banter between them. Even when they were teasing one another, they never really meant to hurt.

"Take this lazy lump away with you, we're losing sales with him lounging there," growled Dora's mother. "Look lively, you!" she said, giving Dora a nudge as one of their most important customers, the manager of an expensive flower shop in Mayfair, approached with a view to choosing the blooms which he would be putting on sale the following day.

"Come on, Harry, we're not wanted round here," Lily shouted, tugging her brother's sleeve. She had to shout because there was so much hubbub in the market, with people bawling out prices and the wheels of barrows and trolleys rumbling over the cobbles, the sounds echoing and amplified beneath the high, arched glass roof.

"Count yourself lucky you work at Covent Garden, not Billingsgate. Dora wouldn't want you standing next to her then!" Lily joked. Covent Garden market sold only fruit, flowers and vegetables, but Billingsgate was the fish market, and a fair old whiff it had about it, too – a whiff that got into your hair and into your clothes and even into your skin. Their uncle worked at Billingsgate and even after his Sunday scrub-down, he still smelled of haddock.

"Walk slowly," she told her long-legged brother, "there's something I must tell you. It's not good, but I don't want you saying it's all my fault, 'cos it wasn't!"

"You're not in the family way, are you, Sis?" Harry looked shocked.

"That's not funny," Lily said with a scowl and Harry burst out laughing.

"Calm yourself, Sis, I didn't really think you were a fallen woman. Not yet, anyway."

Lily shot out her right foot and kicked him on the back of the ankle.

"Ouch!" he exclaimed, bending down to rub his bruise. "Out with it, then," he prompted. "We're nearly home."

"I've lost my job. I was singing and didn't hear some customers come in."

"Typical!" was Harry's instant response. Then, seeing how upset Lily looked, he suggested, "Would you like me to go and see Mr Collyer and see if I can get your job back?"

Lily shook her head, knowing that there was nothing her brother could do but appreciating his gallantry. "He wouldn't have me back, whatever the circumstances. I was having a terrible time trying to learn all the different types of material, anyway. I wish I could be interested in dress-making like Mother, but I'm not. Clothes don't interest me."

"I can see that," taunted Harry. "You do look pretty awful. What *is* that sack thing you've got draped round you? It looks like a horse-blanket!"

"It's Mrs Molloy's shawl," Lily informed him, spluttering with laughter.

"So what are you going to do now? Find a rich man and marry him?"

"Not on your nellie!" Lily retorted.

"Shall I see if there's anything going in the market? Fancy shelling peas?"

"Imagine what Mother would say!" Lily fell silent for a moment, wondering whether or not to confide in her brother. He might promise not to say anything to Mother, but she couldn't trust him not to let something slip if he was drinking beer with Father. He'd think it was a joke, but she knew that if they found out she was singing for money, they would view it as nothing short of prostitution!

People outside the entertainment world automatically thought that actresses and singers were wicked women who led sinful lives and were definitely not admitted into polite drawing-rooms. If she were to be found out, her parents might shun her and disown her and then she would be forced to live the way Billy Morgan did, dossing ten to a kitchen floor in somebody's rooms, or sleeping in a paupers' shelter.

"Penny for them," Harry said, noticing her quietness.

"Oh, nothing," she said. "Mother's got one of her head-aches. I was worrying about her, hoping she was feeling better now."

Harry came out with the thought which had entered Lily's mind time after time. "If only she hadn't had Archie…"

"Yes, if only," Lily agreed.

Charlie Cobbett rolled in at around eleven o'clock, well oiled with ale. As he clumped up the stairs, his tin whistle fell out of his pocket and clattered all the way down to the bottom. Lily, lying awake next to her mother who was nursing Archie, heard her father issue a loud swear word. A door banged open and angry words came from one of the other residents who had been woken by the row.

"Cecily! Cecily?" Charlie called as he entered their flat. Actually, Lily thought, it sounded more like "Sheshily".

Lily's mother sighed, got out of bed, draped a shawl around her shoulders and took Archie into the other room.

Lily heaved a sigh of relief and settled down to get some sleep. Just as oblivion was descending, she heard her father burst into raucous laughter and heard her name mentioned.

"That's our Lily!" he said. "Where is the girl? Hey, Lily, let's have a song!"

Lily heard her mother trying to shush him up before the neighbours started banging on the walls, but he refused to be silenced and the next minute, a merry tune was being piped on his tin whistle. The door banged open and her father stood there, dancing a jig on the spot as he played. He beckoned to her, took his mouth away from the mouthpiece of the whistle long enough to say, "Come on, lass, sing!" and resumed playing.

Lily smiled. Despite her tiredness, she couldn't fail to respond to music, and her father was exceptionally skilled on his whistle. He owned four, all in different keys. This one was in the key of G, which suited her voice the best.

He started to play the old Scottish song, *Maire's Wedding*, and she joined in with the words. "Step we gaily, on we go, Heel for heel and toe for toe." She stood on the bed, danced a few steps, then fell over in a tangle of bedclothes.

"Hey! I'm trying to sleep!" Harry's protest came from the kitchen, into which he had dragged his blankets.

Their father pulled a funny face and carried on playing. It was *Paddy McGinty's Goat* now, which always made Lily laugh as she sang about the Irishman who had gone out to buy a nanny goat and had ended up with a billy goat instead, causing all the ladies of Killaloo to place pillows under their skirts in case the nasty male goat butted them.

Suddenly, Charlie danced a little too energetically,

caught his heel against the chest of drawers and fell over. Lily shrieked with laughter and even Mother and Harry laughed when they came in to see what had happened.

That was the end of that night's entertainment. Mother insisted on putting Charlie to bed and she stayed in the room with him. Harry went back to the kitchen floor and Lily had the unaccustomed luxury of a bed – and a room – to herself, a room which was blessedly Archie-free.

Mother was in a good mood the next morning and announced that her headache had gone. She even tried to cheer Lily up – not that she needed cheering. "Don't worry, lovey," she said soothingly, "it's not the end of the world, losing your job. We'll all do our best to find you another one. When I see Mrs Booth-Edwards this afternoon, I'll ask her if she knows of any openings."

Lily's mother was an excellent dressmaker. She had just a few clients, recommended by other ladies for whom she had made outfits, but they were loyal even if they only had one dress made per season.

Lily had once asked her mother why she didn't advertise, pointing out that she could get lots more work then. Her mother had explained that her eyesight was not what it once was and that too much straining over tiny stitches in a poor light would give her more headaches. Also, she would need a proper work room and they couldn't afford one.

"I would love to have a proper dressmaking establishment, away from these poor rooms," Cecily said longingly. "Can you imagine having clients visiting me here! What would they think? They might be worried that their new dresses would have fleas!"

Although Lily laughed along with her mother, at the core of her was a sense of pity, and shame. If only Father didn't drink so much, they wouldn't have to live like this. They could have a whole house to themselves, with a garden and a suite of rooms for her mother's business.

Lily's mind floated off into her favourite daydream again. If she were to make a success of busking, perhaps she could save up so much money that they *could* have a house and a garden! It was all down to her.

"I think I'll go out and take a turn around the block, get some fresh air," she said, reaching for her coat and her hat. She hated wearing hats, but no respectable woman would be seen outdoors without one. So she placed the battered creation of straw and imitation flowers on her head and pinned it in place.

Her mother handed her a coin. "Could you go to the baker's and buy us a milk loaf?" she asked.

A milk loaf was a bit more expensive than some of the other kinds of bread, but it was very nourishing and nourishment was what her mother needed at the moment.

"Of course," replied Lily.

"Don't be too long," her mother instructed. "I'd like you to clean and tidy while I'm out."

Lily's heart sank. "I'll be back in half an hour," she promised. She had hoped to escape for a couple of hours at least, but now her perambulations would be cut short. Still, she knew exactly where to find the person she was looking for...

Jago Jagger, king of the buskers, was at his usual window table in Dawson's Coffee House in the Strand. He was reading *The Times* and pretending to be a gentleman, but no London gentleman ever sported a dark grey suit with a lavender waistcoat and light grey bowler, hat, and wore his whiskers in such a clumpy fashion that he had two half-beards travelling down the sides of his face to his chin, with nothing connecting them in the middle other than a bristling band of moustache.

It was to Jago that every would-be busker had to report, if he knew what was good for him. Jago controlled many of the busking pitches and kept a detailed appointments book and saw to it that there were never any clashes between buskers, as unseemly fights over a pitch would ruin the busking trade. So Billy Morgan would play the Old Mo at seven and someone else would turn up with an instrument or performing monkey to entertain the second house.

In return for such diligent organization, Jago would take a cut of each performer's revenue. Sometimes he would even perform himself, with his famous one-man-band routine involving a drum, cymbals, whistles, a ukelele and a parrot. He had been quite famous as a young man, before rheumatics had set in and stiffened his fingers and he had decided to control the pitches he had once played.

As his "patch" covered theatreland from Covent Garden to Oxford Street and the Strand, Jago was a wealthy man indeed. Rumour had it that he kept a mistress in Bath, as well as a wife and six children in Bow.

Jago would expect Lily to audition for him. If he didn't think her performance up to scratch, he would ban her from busking outside the theatres and she would be forced to seek a pitch outside a shop, or hover around the theatre queues and take her chances as an unofficial entertainer who was likely to be chased off by the regular pitch holders.

She hovered nervously outside the coffee house, her ears deafened by the rumbling traffic, her body jostled by the press of people hurrying along the pavement, all intent on some private errand. All at once, her resolution stiffened. This won't do, she told herself firmly. Pushing the door of the coffee house open, she stepped inside.

Instantly, heads turned, unused to the sight of an un-chaperoned young lady inside such an establishment. Coffee house *habitués* were mainly men, although there was a table containing four women, all talking animatedly over a pile of pamphlets.

Lily halted beside Jago Jagger's table. "Mr Jagger?" she said politely.

"Huh?" grunted the short, barrel-chested man. His hairy head turned on the thick, almost non-existent neck which was sunk into the high collar of his shirt.

"Mr Jagger, I ... I would like to become a busker."

"*You?*" Jagger barked, then flung back his head and roared with laughter. "Go back home to your mother, dearie. Busking's not for the likes of tender young girls like you. It's for tough people who don't mind catcalls and improper suggestions. You look as if the faintest criticism would reduce you to tears – and that's not entertaining people, is it? You'd be out in all weathers, too. A thin, delicate little thing like you would be dead of pneumonia before winter's out."

He turned back to his newspaper and ignored her.

Lily's chin shot up. "I'm not a delicate little thing," she

protested. "And with a father and brother working in the market, I've heard all the bad language there is. I'm tougher than I look. Here, I'll prove it!"

Taking up a cheeky stance, one hand on her hip and one index finger touching her chin, she rolled her eyes roguishly and, adopting a childish lisp, started to sing a song Billy had taught her, one of Marie Lloyd's risqué hits.

After just a few lines, Jagger started to grin and Lily knew she had won over her audience. Without a break, she went straight from that to a song which was a complete contrast, a tear-jerking lament about a man whose wife had died in childbirth, leaving him all alone with a tiny baby. As she sang, she felt sure she could see Jagger's eyes growing wet and shiny.

She bowed her head on the last tragic note and applause and cries of "Bravo!" rang out from around the coffee house. She looked up at Jago Jagger, whose ruddy face bore a wistful expression in place of its normal belligerent stare. "Well?" she enquired.

Jago made no immediate answer but when he fished in his pocket and brought out the famous leather-bound notebook, Lily knew she had succeeded.

"What's your name?" he asked her.

"Lily Cobbett."

"Well, Lily Cobbett," he said, scribbling her name down in his notebook, "you can have twenty minutes at the Tivoli at two o'clock this afternoon for a try-out, then tonight, seven o'clock, you can have the tail-ender slot at the Oxford."

Lily gasped with delight. She knew from Billy what a tail-ender meant. The main busker stood at the front of the queue doing his act. The tail-ender stood at the back, catching the newcomers as they arrived. A tail-ender didn't make so much money, but there was always a large crowd at the Oxford and lots of money to be made.

"Thank you, thank you!" she said and, impulsively, leaned over and kissed Jago's hairy cheek.

As she whisked away, he called after her, "Good luck!"

When Lily left the coffee house, her eye was caught by the clock above a jeweller's shop across the street. "Oh goodness!" she muttered out loud. She had been far longer than the half hour she had promised her mother and she hadn't even been to the baker's yet. What if they were sold out of milk loaves?

They were. Lily guiltily paid for a cob loaf instead and made a silent promise to her mother that once she was a successful busker, she would have as many milk loaves as she wanted, every day.

Chapter 4

"Please, Mrs Molloy? Just for an hour? I must go out. I've simply *got* to!"

The homely Irishwoman couldn't resist the appeal of the young girl in the patched dress, holding baby Archie in her arms. Mrs Molloy felt quite cross with Lily's mother. She could sew, everyone knew that, so why didn't she make more clothes for her children? What Mrs Molloy didn't know, of course, was that, owing to Cecily Cobbett's poor eyesight, every extra stitch she sewed was likely to bring on one of her fearsome headaches, so her sewing was limited to that which earned her money, for which it was worth suffering a migraine.

Mrs Molloy held out her arms for the heavy baby and it was with a light heart that Lily tripped down to the Tivoli in the Strand – a heart which immediately sank when she saw the noisy, enthusiastic crowd which was already gathering for the Saturday matinée. Braying young men and screeching girls, men who had already quaffed too much ale and were sullying the air with coarse jokes. How would she ever gain the attention of such people and get them to listen to her? How would she ever make herself heard above the hubbub of traffic and excited chatter?

If only I had an eye-catching costume to wear, she thought.

In the grey skirt and white, high-necked blouse she had worn for her work at the drapery shop, and her old blue coat which her mother had tried to update by sewing some brown fur on to the collar and cuffs, she looked every inch the shop girl which she had been.

A surge of panic made her heart somersault in her chest. *I'm going home*, she thought. *I can't do this on my own. With Billy, yes, but not on my own. I'm going now!*

Then she remembered how she had steeled herself to confront Jago that morning and how she had sung in front of an entire coffee-house full of strangers. She had convinced Jago that she would not be scared off by ribald comments and heckling – that she was strong and spirited and capable. What would he think if he found out that she had run off like a frightened rabbit at her first sight of her very own theatre queue?

The reedy sound of a fiddle arrested her ears. A ragged man had taken his position at the front of the crowd that was supposed to be hers alone. *How dare he!* she thought indignantly.

"Hey!" she called, running up to him. "This is my pitch. You get to the tail-end!"

A few people overheard the altercation and looked their way with interest. She had their attention. It was now or never. She opened her mouth and began to sing, but what came out was little more than a squeak and nobody so much as looked her way.

Oh no, she thought, *they can't hear me, I'll have to sing louder*. But she couldn't. Nervousness was robbing her lungs of their usual power. Lily closed her eyes, imagining Billy was at her side, conjuring up the sound of his accordion. Immediately, her spirits improved and she began to sing with gusto. There was a flutter of applause and a few comments reached her ears.

"I say, what a pretty little songbird," one paunchy man said. "Do you think she'll squeak if I pinch her?"

"Not half as much as you'll squeak if I kick you where I'm thinking of!" Lily instantly retorted. It was the sort of remark she would make to her brother and it simply tripped off her tongue, but it pleased those within earshot, who shouted with laughter.

This matinée crowd was light-hearted, they were out for jollity. No use singing them tragic dirges, thought Lily, and she searched her memory for every humorous and saucy song she knew. Coins kept clinking on to the piece of old velvet she had laid in front of her feet. Her throat was growing hoarse but shouts of, "Encore! More, more!" kept her going.

When after twenty minutes her replacement approached, Lily couldn't switch off her delighted smile. She curtseyed gracefully and gathered up her money. "Thank you, you've been a lovely audience," she called out, as if she were on a real stage in a real theatre.

"Thanks for warming them up for me," said the busker who was replacing her, a swarthy man with a banjo under his arm.

"Huh!" Lily snorted, detecting sarcasm in his tone. So he didn't take her seriously. Well, she'd show him! "Here comes Dan Joe with his banjo," she carolled, and hopped round the annoyed man, inventing words as she went along and miming strumming a banjo.

The crowd laughed and jeered at the man.

"Go home, banjo player," one man shouted. "Give us back our little lady in blue. She can really sing."

Lily was thrilled to hear his words. So they really had liked her!

"Your turn now," she said to the man. "You're right, I've warmed them up good and proper."

He glared and, as he began to strum the banjo's rattly strings, the crowd turned back to their friends and ignored him.

Lily tied a knot in the piece of velvet, holding her money tight and secure. She placed the clinking bundle inside her coat and buttoned up around it. Folding her arms in front of her, she hurried up Southampton Street, seeing the glass roof of the market ahead reflecting the watery blue of the wintry sky.

She was so wrapped in the glow of her success, and the excitement of having earned her heavy bag of money, that she didn't at first hear somebody call her name.

"Lily! Lily Cobbett." It was Jago Jagger, panting to catch up with her. "Aren't you forgetting something?" he said.

Lily frowned and gave him a puzzled look. "I don't know what you mean," she said.

"My cut." He caught up with her and stood in front of her, blocking her path. "Come on, count it out."

"What? Here?" There were people all around. If she started counting the money now, surely some urchin or vagabond would snatch it!

"Everyone knows me. They won't dare to steal it. Now, come on, you know the arrangement. Ten per cent," he said sternly.

Lily handed the bag to him, in too much of a daze to

add it up herself. "You count it for me, please," she said.

Jagger did so. He extracted three silver coins and pocketed them. "Here you are," he said, handing the rest back. "You did well this afternoon. They liked you. But you must come to the coffee house and find me tonight when you've finished – if I or my helpers don't find you first."

"Who are your helpers? I'm not going to hand money over to a stranger, I might give it to the wrong person," Lily said anxiously.

"There are three of them: Titch, Stan and Col. They all carry one of these."

From his waistcoat pocket, Jago pulled a silver medallion. It was engraved with a portrait of Jago himself on one side and a harp on the other. "To symbolize music," he explained, as if it wasn't obvious. "I only had four of them made. If a helper leaves, he has to hand it in or God help him!"

Jago drew his hand sideways across his throat in a murderous gesture which made Lily gasp and take a step back. "Don't worry, little lassie, I've never killed a man. Not *personally*," he added meaningfully. Then, with a "Don't forget tonight," he swung his meaty shoulders into the crowd and was gone.

Lily was tempted to dawdle on the way home. She had money, she could buy herself something nice. Or a present for her mother. But her fear at carrying that amount of money on her when some rapscallion might have witnessed their transaction in Southampton Street made Lily clutch her arms even more tightly around herself and hurry for home. She knew that buying things this early in her busking career might be a mistake as they would be bound to raise questions at home about where the money had come from. Best to hide it for a while, and then pretend to have a legitimate job somewhere...

But singing *was* a legitimate job, she reasoned. What was so terrible and sinful about it? She remembered a book she had read – one of the so-called Penny Dreadfuls, romantic storybooks which were published by the score. This one had concerned a titled young lady who had been tricked out of her inheritance by her father's caddish nephew. She had joined a group of players and had played the piano and sung at concert parties, and had consequently been banished by so-called "polite society". However, the timely presence of a rich Italian count in one of her audiences, and his consequent offer of marriage, had saved her tarnished reputation, even though the young lady had never been so much as kissed by a man.

It was ridiculous, Lily thought. Why should being an entertainer introduce you to situations which were any more risky than in any other walk of life? Surely a girl's reputation could be just as compromised by her behaviour at a ball? The trouble was that those female entertainers who *did* lead a wild life got talked about and consequently everyone thought that all girls who were on the stage behaved in the same way. It simply wasn't fair.

But of course, being in the public eye did bring many admirers your way, Lily realized. "Stage door Johnnies", they were called. Beaux who waited after the performance with flowers and invitations for their favourite girl singer or dancer. The thought of being courted in this way was quite exciting. Not that it would happen to her. What rich, titled gentleman was likely to want to court an unfashionably dressed busker with only two equally shabby coats to her name? She had no clothes in which to go out to dine in an expensive restaurant; no clothes she could wear to visit a country house, or go to the opera and the races, all the things rich people did.

The money jingled enticingly beneath her coat. *Soon*, she thought to herself, *soon...*

Although getting out of the house that afternoon had been a simple matter, escaping in the evening wasn't nearly so easy. At least she didn't have the added complication of having to smuggle out a musical instrument. That was a relief, she thought as she racked her brains to invent an excuse.

Fate provided one in the form of Mrs Booth-Edwards. Her mother, looking harassed, said she had a favour to ask of Lily.

"I don't know if she will like the collar I've put on this dress. It isn't what she asked for but Collyers had run out of the type of lace she wanted. Would you please take her the dress and show it to her, Lily? She needs it for a musical supper next Wednesday and if I don't finish it, she may cancel her other orders. Then I'll have to take in washing like Mrs Molloy. You wouldn't want a washerwoman for a mother, now would you?"

Lily did her best to look grave and to hide the delighted smile that was trying to tweak up the corners of her mouth. Cecily Cobbett didn't know it, but she was giving her daughter exactly the excuse she needed.

The journey to Mrs Booth-Edwards' house in Brook Street would take about half an hour on foot. Half an hour there, half an hour back and any amount of waiting time, as Mrs Booth-Edwards might not be at home, or might be busy. Lily would have to leave the dress with her personal maid and come back later for the verdict on it. Oh, it was perfect!

"Of course I'll go for you, Mother," she said. "And I hope Mrs Booth-Edwards likes it."

Her mother handed her the dress, wrapped in brown paper and tied loosely with string. "I've folded it very carefully, so please try not to crush it," her mother said.

"I won't," promised Lily.

"If only you had taken after me and had some skill with the sewing needle," Mrs Cobbett sighed. "You could have been such a help to me, now that my eyes are not so good. We might have started our own fashion business. We might have got rich!"

Her mother's eyes turned upwards, dreamily, unseeingly, as she envisioned a rosy, impossible alternative life. It suddenly struck Lily how alike she and her mother were in this respect. They were both dreamers – although she, Lily, was determined to turn her personal dream into reality. Indeed, she had already started, as the small collection of coins beneath the loose floorboard under her bed proved, each time she lifted the wood to gloat over its glint.

She was walking briskly along Endell Street when she spied Billy Morgan. He was on the other side of the road, travelling in the same direction as herself, his accordion on his back.

He saw her and waved. "Where are you going?" he shouted.

"On an errand for my mother," Lily yelled back.

"Let me walk with you," he called, and crossed the road.

The clock on the mantelpiece had said twenty-five past five when she had left home. Billy would have to get to his pitch outside the Old Mo by a quarter to seven, so there was no chance of him discovering her secret destination, the Oxford. "Please do," she accepted.

He was so tall now. Girls gave him bold glances as he and Lily passed by. She felt proud of having him by her side, and as jealous as if he had been her sweetheart. If only... But he had never given her any hint that he liked her in that way.

She chatted about the dress, and about Mrs Booth-Edwards. When they reached Brook Street, Lily told Billy, "You mustn't come to the door with me. Somebody might see and tell my mother."

Surely it must be time for Billy to depart for Drury Lane? The queue for the Old Mo started forming at six-thirty. If he didn't leave now and walk smartly, he would miss his slot and another busker would steal it! Thinking that perhaps he hadn't looked at a clock recently, Lily said urgently, "Billy, it must be after six. Hadn't you better be going?"

Billy laughed. "No, Lily, it's not the Old Mo for me tonight. I need a change of audience. I want to sing to a crowd who haven't heard all my songs before. I've got it all arranged. Tonight, I'm going to try the Oxford."

Chapter 5

Lily thought she was going to faint. Everything swirled around her and the chimney-pots on the tall, narrow houses seemed to be crashing down on to her head.

"Lily? Are you all right, Lily?"

Billy took hold of her arm in concern. Normally, she would have experienced a whole realm of pleasant emotions – Billy had never held her arm like that before – but right then, all she could feel was utter panic and alarm. The Oxford… How could it be? That meant she couldn't possibly sing there tonight! It meant no more coins going into her meagre store. It also meant that Jago Jagger might send his boys looking for her, wondering why she hadn't paid her percentage, and if she said she hadn't sung after all, he might not believe her.

"I'm quite all right," she assured him. "I just looked up at the roofs too quickly and felt dizzy."

"I'm worried about you. You may be ill," he said. "Get your errand done and I'll wait here and see you safely home."

She didn't want to be seen safely home, but what alternative did she have?

By the time a maid had answered and Lily had explained her errand and handed over the package, She had formulated an idea – one she put into practice as soon as she rejoined Billy.

"Let me come to the Oxford with you," she said. "I'll sing with you and if there's no tail-ender, I could do that, too, and earn a bit of money for Mother. She's very short since I lost my job. You know where all Father's money goes. She says that if she can't pay the rent next week, we'll be thrown out by the landlady and we'll have to go and live in Seven Dials."

It was an invention – she couldn't imagine jolly Mrs Molloy throwing them out for being just one week overdue with the rent – but nevertheless, she gave a dramatic shudder at the thought of that overcrowded slum, with its strings of ragged washing flapping across the alleys, its hordes of grubby, screaming children, pickpockets all, the mangy, yapping curs, the fights and even murders which occurred with frequency. It was all on her doorstep, just yards down the road, a nightmare reminder of what happened to people who had sunk almost as low as they could get.

"You won't get thrown out," Billy said cheerfully. "Harry has a job. Surely he's bringing money home?"

"Harry also has a girlfriend," Lily said darkly. She had seen him giving Dora a trinket he had bought in the market, so he certainly wasn't handing over all the money he could.

"Doesn't Edward send any money home?" Billy asked.

"It's been eight months since we heard from him," Lily admitted. "He was in the Dutch East Indies then. He could be anywhere by now."

"Well, I only have myself to worry about. If I don't earn, I don't eat," Billy said.

"If I don't earn, *three* of us don't eat – me, Mother and Archie," Lily said, then frowned as Billy started laughing. "I don't see anything amusing in what I just said," she challenged him.

"It's Archie. I had a sudden vision of him tucking into a great big porterhouse steak," he said.

Lily remembered having grumbled to Billy about her constantly whining baby brother. He was no doubt wondering why she was showing such concern about his welfare all of a sudden. She didn't want him to start asking probing questions, so instead she let herself smile at his joke, then said, "Come on, let's get down to the Oxford."

Lily's ruse worked. She sang a couple of songs with Billy to get the people interested and start the coins landing in the hat, then she moved to the back of the queue, where it was so noisy that Billy's accordion could hardly be heard at all.

It was a damp, misty night with the thick, tarry smell of coal fires in the air. A tune from the North-East came to her, a plaintive song called *The Oggie Man*, an oggie being a local kind of hot pasty.

"The rain is gently falling and the oggie man's not here…" she sang.

"Give the lassie a penny so she can buy one o' them oggies. She looks 'alf-starved," said a woman, nudging her husband.

Chuckles broke out around them, but Lily sang serenely on. Sad songs weren't meant to be interrupted to deal with hecklers and respond to comments. In any case, when she sang any kind of tender or sensitive song, she became totally lost in it. Which was why she didn't notice two men who, quite separately, were staring at her intently.

One was middle-aged, in a smart grey suit and overcoat. He had light brown hair and a moustache. The other was tiny, almost dwarflike. He had a crooked back and one shoulder was raised in a hunch. Despite his disabilities, he was dapperly dressed with a pink carnation in his button-hole and a little, pointy, neatly-trimmed beard.

Judging that one wistful song was enough, Lily switched to a rollicking sea shanty and the crowd tapped, clapped and whistled an accompaniment. Lily knew she had them eating out of her hand now. She looked towards Billy, who gave a thumbs-up gesture and grinned at her.

At the end of her impromptu performance, she brought out her faded piece of damson-coloured velvet and toured the back section of the crowd, holding it out for their con-tributions. There were quite a few. During this task, the man in the overcoat disappeared but the little hunchback remained.

Billy surrendered his pitch to the next street enter-tainers, a fire-eater and his accomplice, and rejoined Lily. Then he saw the little man.

"Evening, Titch!" he called.

So *that* was the Titch whom Jago had mentioned, thought Lily. She would certainly recognize *him* again.

Billy dutifully counted their coins and handed over the amount due, which Titch pocketed with a cheeky grin. He looked like a monkey, thought Lily – a monkey in human clothes. He had those deep-set brown eyes that monkeys had, and little hands like paws, and scampering feet. But instinct told her that he would make a dangerous pet. Jago wouldn't have a henchman who couldn't look after himself.

Titch gave Lily a curious glance, then trotted off at a remarkable pace towards his next collection post. Billy smiled – a smile that was like warming cold hands in front of a roaring fire.

"I'll walk with you back to Brook Street, if you like," he offered.

Lily suddenly found a great wave of shyness washing over her. *Stop it at once, you stupid girl!* she chided herself. *This isn't a sweetheart, it's just your old friend Billy. You mustn't act this way with him.*

She may have made up her mind on that point, but her body was disobeying her. It was full of tremors and chills and hot and cold shivers – especially when Billy took her elbow to help her across the street.

As they walked, Lily felt she needed to clear the air and put Billy off the scent. Oh, it was all so awkward. She had honestly thought that he was going to stick to the Old Mo pitch for ever and that she could sing anywhere else and Billy would never know. But imagine what would happen if he asked Jago for a pitch at the Alhambra, or the Tivoli, and found that she had already been given it! It would be the end of their friendship, the end of her hopes of something more than friendship developing between them.

"I … I hope you didn't mind about tonight," she said cautiously. "I hope you don't think I was taking money out of your pocket…"

"If you hadn't done it, someone else would have done, and I'd far rather it was you," he said gallantly. "Did you hear them talking about you? They were all saying what a wonderful voice you have and it's true. Tell you what, why don't you and I team up on a regular basis? Sing together as a double act? You know how good we sound together."

Lily sucked in her lower lip and bit it. "I, er … well, what about the money?" she asked. "If we split it, you wouldn't get enough to live on."

"You would still have something to take back to your mother, though," Billy pointed out. "Something is always better than nothing." He grinned his irrepressible, twinkling grin, but all Lily felt was guilt.

"No," she said, "it's better as it is. I'll just sing a couple of songs with you occasionally, to help you out."

"That's my girl! You'd never survive as a busker, anyway. You're too ladylike," Billy said.

His words inflamed her pride. She felt like running straight back to the theatre crowd and singing one of Marie Lloyd's most ribald numbers. Instead, she nodded and pretended to agree with him.

At Brook Street, Mrs Booth-Edwards' personal maid handed Lily back the parcel containing the dress, now not nearly so neatly wrapped. "Madam says it won't do," sniffed the maid. "She asked for Belgian lace in the snowflake pattern, and Belgian lace is what she wants. Your mother is to provide it and have the dress ready on Tuesday."

"Tuesday?" burst out Lily. "But she told my mother Wednesday!"

"Then she must have changed her mind."

The door closed in Lily's face with a loud slam. Lily felt tears welling in her eyes. "M-Mother can't finish that dress. She can't get the lace. And she can't w-work quickly any more, her eyes are bad," Lily stammered through the teardrops which were now streaming down her face.

She dashed the cuff of her coat across her eyes. Then she

felt Billy's fingertip gently brushing a fresh tear from her eyelashes.

"Poor Lily," he whispered. "I'm sure it's not impossible. I'm sure that between the two of you, you can find the right lace and get the dress made. I'll help if I can."

"Thank you, Billy," Lily said gratefully. She didn't like to admit that she couldn't sew. No man wanted a wife who was no good with a needle.

A *wife*? What was she thinking of? How had that word popped into her head? She was never going to wed. Never!

Her heart felt like a runaway horse galloping beneath her ribs. Her eyelid could still feel the soft dab of his fingertip. Her lips were trembling so much, it was a wonder that she had been able to form the words to thank him. *Oh, Billy Morgan,* she thought, *what are you doing to me?*

"I'll be at the Oxford again tomorrow," Billy told her. "Can you come?"

"I'll see," she said as they parted in Endell Street. "I may not be able to come out, though, what with the dress and everything…"

"Then I'll see you when I see you, Lily."

He seized one of Lily's hands and pressed warm, dry lips against the back of it. Lily gasped and almost dropped her precious parcel in a puddle. "Billy Morgan!" she exclaimed.

"That's me!" He blew her a kiss and waved as he went off down the street.

Lily was still standing there attempting to collect herself when she heard footsteps running up behind her and a panting voice cry, "Aha! Caught you!"

There, with his cheeks flushed and his eyes sparkling with mischief and triumph, was her brother Harry.

Chapter 6

For the second time that day, Lily wished the ground could open and swallow her up. She couldn't issue a word in her defence. All she could do was open and close her mouth like a stranded fish gasping for air.

"So, my dear sister, who is he? What is his name? He looked a rum sort of fellow to me, some sort of gypsy with that concertina affair on his back. Don't tell me you're mixing with the circus folk, or the travelling players? What will Mother say when she hears about these goings-on of yours?"

The word "Mother" was enough to restore Lily's vocal cords. "Please don't say anything to Mother! Promise me, Harry, please! Mother is in a lot of trouble and I don't wish to add to it. She can't finish this dress and it's needed by Tuesday. I don't want her worrying over me as well."

"Then, as your older brother, you must tell me all," Harry insisted. "I have a right to know."

Lily's cheeks flushed with anger. Harry had no more right to know what she got up to with Billy, or any other young man, than she had to know what he did with his girlfriends. But he thought he did, and she knew he wouldn't stop goading her until he got the truth out of her.

She took a deep breath and tried to calm down. "It's not

the way it might have looked," she said. "His name is Billy Morgan and he is a talented musician. He works as a busker, playing to the theatre queues."

"So he's one of the nuisances who makes such a tuneless row outside Drury Lane," snorted Harry.

Lily leapt to Billy's defence. "Billy isn't tuneless. He's very clever and writes his own songs, the words and the music. I met him when I stopped and listened to him one day. He was so good that I sought him out again, so I could hear some more. He's got a beautiful voice, Harry. You should listen to him sometime. Tonight, he saw me walking to Brook Street and asked if he could escort me. I felt it was safer to have a companion for my walk, than to walk alone, so I accepted."

Harry's brow knitted into a frown. "And you didn't think about what that acceptance might mean to him? That it might be a signal to him that you would consider him as a sweetheart?"

Colour flamed afresh in Lily's cheeks. "Certainly not!" she snapped. "Why should half an hour spent talking about music make him think that?"

"Because you've given him encouragement. Look at the way he kissed your hand! I saw everything. That young man is in love with you now, Lily. You'll never get rid of him unless you tell him quite plainly that you don't want anything to do with him. In fact, if I see him again, I'll do it for you. I'll warn him off, as your brother."

How dare you? fumed Lily, but she kept her thoughts to herself. Harry was quite right. She *had* been too free with Billy. But Harry didn't appear to consider that there was another type of relationship possible between a girl and a boy, apart from that of sweethearts. It was possible to be friends – just friends.

"I suppose you told him you like singing, too," Harry bumbled on, uncannily getting closer and closer to the truth. "The next thing you know, he'll be asking you to sing with him, encouraging you to become a busker, too. You mark my words!"

Lily glanced away, staring across the street so that her guilty expression should not betray her. Then, composing herself, she turned back to her brother and looked him straight in the eye, knowing that if she didn't manage to set his mind at rest now, she might never be allowed out on her own again.

"I can assure you," she said, her eyes boring unwaveringly into his, "that I am *not* in love with Billy Morgan, never have been, never shall be, and that I have no intention of encouraging him."

Harry shrugged. "All right, I believe you. Better be getting home to Mother, I suppose."

"Yes," said Lily, euphoric with relief.

But her high spirits were dampened by her mother's reaction to the news that the collar had to be of Belgian lace, and the dress had to be finished a day early. Cecily gave a loud moan and covered her face with her hands.

"Mother!" cried Lily in alarm.

Her mother removed her hands and gave her a look which was both weary and utterly defeated. In the flickering light from the oil lamp hanging on the wall, she looked twenty years older than her forty-five years. "It's no good, Lily," she said, tears throbbing in her voice. "You see, it wasn't true that Collyers didn't have that lace. They did, but it was much too expensive and since Old Man Collyer asked you to leave, Lily, he's taken against us Cobbetts and won't give me credit like he used to. There's nothing I can do."

"Harry?" Lily fixed her brother with a gimlet eye. "Surely you can give a few shillings to help Mother?"

Harry's face bore a frozen, horrified look, rather as if someone had just nailed his feet to the floor. He turned out all his pockets but there was nothing in them save a few pennies and lumps of fluff. He had spent all his money on ale and Dora, that much was obvious. And tomorrow was Sunday when no work was done.

"How about Father?" Lily ventured.

"Huh! *Him!*" their mother scoffed. "If I had a penny for every pint of brown ale your father has drunk in his lifetime, I'd be a very rich woman. He's given me a few shillings towards the rent so it's no use asking for any more. I bet he's run up a slate with every publican from Shadwell to the Elephant!"

The coins in their velvet bag were burning against her body, searing her with guilt. She couldn't produce them now. Too many questions would be asked. But on Monday ... why, on Monday afternoon she could tell her mother she had earned a bit of money running errands for the baker, or writing letters for one of the offices round about, and then the lace could be bought.

But the dress was needed on Tuesday. Her mother would need all Monday to work on it. All tomorrow, too. Oh, what was she to do?

She glanced at the clock. Along Oxford Street and Regent Street some of the big shops stayed open until late

53

on a Saturday evening. Crowds thronged to them, attracted by the flickering glow of the gas lamps and the cries of the costers outside, their barrows selling everything from flowers to boot polish. She had to go there now and see if there was anywhere she could buy that very special lace. It was her only chance.

"Excuse me a moment, Mother ... Harry." Lily went into the other room, tiptoeing so as not to wake the baby. She quietly lifted the loose floorboard and took out the money which she had placed in the papier-mâché box which used to be home to her brooches and hairpins. She took out some coins to supplement what she had earned that evening and tied it all up in the piece of velvet. She then found a length of ribbon and tied her moneybag around her waist. If she kept her arms folded in front of her, there would be no tell-tale jingle.

Telling her mother she was going "downstairs", which was the family term for seeing if the backyard lavatory was free, Lily went out of the house. She half thought that she might bump into Billy again, but she didn't. As she threaded her way through the West End crowds, people hardly noticed the drably dressed girl slipping past them like a shadow. She found what she was looking for, a rich array of shimmering cloth in a shop window, and boldly went inside.

A salesgirl turned up her nose, then turned away and ignored Lily, obviously thinking she was a poor girl come in just to admire the wonderful materials. Lily cleared her throat and the girl snapped, "Yes, Miss, what can I do for you?", looking at Lily as if she were a piece of dirt.

Just you wait! Lily thought. One day she would be rich and she and her servants would sweep in here and finger every length of cloth. Then, just when she had this snooty girl panting for her massive order, she would say, "Oh, what a poor selection, let us go elsewhere," and leave without buying anything! It was a most satisfying fantasy.

"Have you got any Belgian lace in this design?" Lily asked, as imperiously as a duchess. She showed her the piece of paper on which Mrs Booth-Edwards had drawn the pattern she wanted.

"It's very expensive," the girl said suspiciously.

"I know that," replied Lily impatiently. "I have the money."

Still looking dubious, the shop assistant went into a back room and returned with a length of the lace. She cut off the amount specified by Lily and handed it to her. When she announced the price, Lily counted out the coins. This shop was more expensive than Collyers and she only just had enough. Her money bag felt very flat and light as she fastened her coat again.

Giving the shop girl a look equally as disdainful as the one that she had given her, Lily swept out of the draper's and set out for home as fast as she could. *If only I could sew,* she thought wistfully as she rushed along. *If only I could make this collar once Mother has gone to sleep. She would wake next day thinking an angel had come down in the night and turned the cheap lace into the best that money can buy!*

But she knew she didn't have the skill to cut and sew the collar. It was all she could do to sew on a button.

When she got home with the lace, she could hear Archie crying again. Her mother was in the kitchen with him, so she stole into the front room where her mother's dressmaking things were kept, found the paper parcel

55

containing the dress, unwrapped a corner and tucked the lace inside. Then she went to find her mother.

"Lily, where *have* you been?" she thundered. "I've been down to Mrs Molloy's looking for you. Where did you get to, girl?"

Lily adopted a vague expression and shook her head. "Nowhere…" she said vaguely. "I just went for a walk, that's all."

"Walk, walk … you're always going for walks. Your feet will drop off one of these days. Sometimes I wonder if—"

Before her mother could start speculating about the purpose of Lily's walks, Lily launched into the brilliant story which occurred to her while walking back. It had to work, it just had to! "I've just remembered something Mrs Booth-Edwards' maid said. It was something about Madam having put something in the parcel for you."

Her mother frowned. "What could it be?"

"Perhaps you'd better open it and find out," said Lily, crossing her fingers behind her back.

Cecily Cobbett's face shone with delight as she undid the parcel. "Look!" she exclaimed. "She's found some snowflake lace for me! She really is my favourite client, you know. She's very kind."

Lily privately thought Mrs Booth-Edwards was a fat, pompous, selfish old woman who thought of nobody but herself, but if thinking she was nice made her mother happy, she was prepared not to voice her opinion.

She watched happily as her mother carefully cut the lace into the right shape for the collar. She helped her to pin it on to the body of the dress. In cold, damp weather like this, her mother's finger joints swelled and ached with rheumatism and she found it difficult to pick up and hold the pins, so Lily did the pinning for her.

The following day, she did all the household chores, too, including cleaning the grate, fetching the water, emptying the slops and preparing the food, to leave her mother free to work on the dress. As usual on a Sunday, Father got in the way. Everywhere she stepped, she fell over his big feet. In the afternoon, Harry said he had a notion to visit sister Edie, who lived with her husband in Cockfosters. Father immediately said that he would go, too, to Lily's great relief.

Once Lily and her mother were alone, Lily helped keep Archie occupied. When dusk fell, she lit the oil lamps and held one so that its light fell on the exact place where her mother was plying her needle. Lily didn't know how she achieved such fine, neat little stitches. They were so small that they were barely visible. Elizabeth had been the only other female in the family to come anywhere close to emulating their mother's needlework skills.

"How much is there still to do?" Lily asked her mother.

"Quite a lot. The side seams are only tacked. Then she wants a lace-trimmed pocket here, and some smocking here … and here. Oh, and bows on both sleeves, just here." Cecily touched the material. "I'll get it done, so long as you're here making yourself useful, and Harry and your father keep out of my way."

"I don't think we'll see them back before midnight," Lily pointed out. "You know what George is like." George, Edie's husband, was famed for the cellar he kept, and for being extremely generous with the contents thereof.

As Lily carefully angled the lamp and fetched whatever

her mother required by way of pins, needles, cotton or scissors, she drifted off into another dream. In it, she and Billy were on a stage in a big theatre. Every seat in the audience was taken, with people packed into the standing area at the back. A tense feeling of anticipation buzzed through the crowd.

Then the curtains opened and the spotlight fell on herself and Billy. He started to sing to her, then dropped to one knee and took her hand, singing, "Will you please be mine?"

Then she started to sing, too, her voice rising gloriously, accepting him. A man dressed as a vicar came on stage and "married" them, to roars of delight from the audience. Then she and Billy sang a wonderful love song together and finally – oh, how this bit set her tingling! – finally, he took her in his arms and kissed her.

Little did Lily guess, but, very soon, part of her dream was destined to come true...

Chapter 7

Next day, on the pretext of continuing her search for work, Lily went to see Jago. She had to explain about Billy, and how the two of them must be kept apart.

He laughed, a deep rumble like the growl of a bulldog. "From what Titch said, I thought the two of you wouldn't *want* to be parted. You sang together like two love-birds, was what Titch said."

"Then Titch was wrong!" Lily snapped.

"Had a lover's tiff, have you?" chuckled Jago, extracting a tin of snuff from his pocket. He opened it, tapped a little of the ginger powder on to his clenched fist, between the base of thumb and forefinger, and put it to his nose. He gave a mighty sniff and snuff dusted his lilac coloured waistcoat. He flicked it with a flourish, replaced the snuff box in his pocket and only then did he take out his book and consult it.

"Billy Morgan is at the Oxford all week," he said. "And now where shall we put you, my little canary bird?"

"I'd prefer not to sing at Drury Lane or the Old Mo – it's too close to home. You see, I don't want my brother or father to find out about my singing. It's a secret," she said. "I'm saving up the money to give them a good Christmas."

It was true. Christmas was just four weeks off and if she didn't provide a Christmas goose or a turkey, then they wouldn't have one at all.

Jago clapped her on the back. "You do that, lass. And do you know what? There just happens to be three days going outside the Alhambra. I'm sure that audience will do you proud."

"Thank you, Jago, thank you!" Lily said, going pink with pleasure.

Jago looked her up and down. "Tell you what," he said. "You can keep all you earn tonight. Put it towards a new dress or coat for yourself, a Christmas present from J.J."

"J.J.?" queried Lily.

"Me – Jago Jagger, of course! Now, get on with you. I have a gentleman waiting to see me."

Lily went, delighted with her progress.

Jago was right about the theatre queues at the Alhambra. They did do Lily proud. And Jago sent her off to matinées at the Tivoli, too. In no time, a whole week went by and she didn't once see Billy. She felt quite despondent. If only she knew where he spent his time when he wasn't singing…

One morning she decided to walk along the Embankment. An icy wind was blowing, carrying the scent of the sea on each buffeting waft. Seagulls were wheeling low and scraping the air with their harsh cries.

Lily walked quickly, hands bunched deep into her pockets as her woollen mittens did little to keep out the bitter cold. The tide was out and the sand exposed. Children and their dogs screamed and played, while men dug around in the muddy sand, looking for coins and any artefacts which they could sell. Sometimes, she had heard, salvage was washed up from sunken boats, and sometimes wonderful old things appeared from the dregs of the river – Roman swords and pottery, bronze jewellery set with precious stones. If only *she* could find one!

She went down one of the sets of wooden steps till her boots touched the gritty sand. Tentatively at first, fearing puddles and quicksand, she set out along the narrow strip of sand. The sound had probably been there for a long time, mingling with the wails of children and gulls, before she heard it: the unmistakable plaintive strains of an accordion.

Billy! she thought, looking all around her. She couldn't see him anywhere. Then she realized the sound came from an old boat, listing at a crazy angle where the receding waters had left it with its keel trapped in the sand. In places its timbers had rotted, but someone had attempted to patch them with board and leathercloth. The music was coming from that boat.

Lily walked gingerly up to it and tapped on the side. With a loud, slow creak, a wooden hatch was lifted and a head popped out.

"Lily! How did you know where I was?" asked Billy's surprised, delighted voice.

"I just came out for a walk by the river and I heard you. It was pure chance," she explained.

"Come aboard. There's just about room for two," he said.

Lily tried, but the angle of the boat made getting on to it difficult, and every time she tried to climb the rough wooden ladder that hung over the side, she trod on the hem of her coat and nearly fell off into the mud. Finally, Billy climbed halfway down the ladder and tugged her on board. He lifted the hatchway so that she could climb down into his dark, cramped, but surprisingly tidy home.

It was pleasantly warm inside the boat. She took off her coat, folded it, placed it in a corner and sat down on a pile of sacks which Billy used for a bed or a seat. An upturned fish box was his table. Daylight filtered in through a small porthole whose glass was sparklingly clean.

"Whose boat is it?" Lily asked.

"There's a man called Jago, who runs the busking pitches around here."

Lily tried not to react. If Billy found out she knew Jago, the game would truly be up!

"She belonged to a friend of his, someone who's left London. Jago said I could live on her, so long as I kept her in good repair. He knows that if nobody keeps an eye on the boat, she'll just rot away, or be set on fire by hooligans. Would you like some tea?"

"Tea?" Lily's eyes opened wide in surprise. "How can you make tea here?" she asked in amazement."

"Easy!" Billy laughed. He took a match and set light to the wick of a small burner. He then produced an oddly shaped metal jug, fat at the bottom and narrow at the top. He dipped it into a bucket of water, then spooned some tea into it, which he took from a wooden box wrapped in oilcloth.

"But that's—" began Lily. She had been going to say, "That's not the way to make tea," but Billy held a finger to his lips and grinned mysteriously. He put the lid on the jug, then placed it on the burner.

"This eez special tea-making machine from ze Far East," he said in a funny accent. Lily laughed. "Actually, it's meant for boiling up coffee in, but it works just as well for tea," he informed her.

The small pot didn't take long to boil. Billy took it off the flame and let it stand while he found two chipped china cups without saucers. He then poured the tea. There was no milk.

"Let it cool before you drink it, otherwise you might burn your mouth," he warned her.

Lily settled down on the heap of sacking. It was cosy in Billy's cabin. The single lamp bathed the tiny compartment in a flickering orange glow. It felt safe and intimate.

Although she was sitting with her knees drawn up under her and her long skirt smoothed over them, she could not have attempted to unwind her legs and change position without her foot coming into contact with Billy, who was sitting on another upturned box, only inches away from her. His eyes closed the gap, gazing into hers with a penetrating intensity which made her flinch, draw back as far as she could, and flush with a throbbing heat. All of a sudden, danger was in the air. She could sense it, almost smell it. Yet Billy was sitting completely still, doing nothing but look at her.

She licked lips which were suddenly dry as paper, and longed for her tea to cool down. "Have ... have you written any new songs lately?" she asked, trying to break the tension.

Billy sighed and shrugged his shoulders. "I have a head full of ideas and no way of writing them down. It's so frustrating. If only you could spend more time with me, Lily, write them down as they come to me."

Lily was about to say that she was only too happy to help him when he sighed again and said, "The trouble is, you couldn't. Inspiration mostly comes to me at impossible hours, like four o'clock."

63

"In the afternoon? That's not too difficult. I—"

Billy interrupted her eager flow of words. "No, I meant four in the morning."

"Oh. I see."

The sense of danger was back in the room again, intensified this time. Lily's heart began to pound as she imagined Billy, lying in his nightshirt beneath his sacking sheets – or maybe he couldn't afford a nightshirt and wore nothing at all! The lamp would be lit, turning his cheekbones and eyesockets to smudges of shadow and his skin to gleaming amber as he began to sing, softly so as not to waken anybody in neighbouring boats, sing the words as they formed, over and over so as to try and impress them on his memory. And then, in the morning's cold light, he would awaken and find his memory held only a sketchy outline of an idea and all of those perfect words had been erased by subsequent dreams and sleep. Oh, the pity of it! The loss. She could weep for him.

There was only one proper answer. She had said it before and now she told him again. "Billy, you need to learn to read and write."

Billy reached out and grasped her hand and she felt her hand leap and struggle beneath his, like a wild creature suddenly trapped. His dark eyes were burning into hers and his colour was high, its flushed radiance emphasizing the sheer chiselled handsomeness of his face, the clear lines of the jawbone, the curve of the high cheekbones, the straight nose.

"Will you help me, Lily? Will you teach me?" he asked her beseechingly.

"If I can," she said. "But you need books…"

"I've got books," Billy said eagerly. He dropped to his knees and lifted the corner of the box he had been sitting on. Beneath it were three books. One was a book of Tennyson's poetry, one a cheap edition of one of Charles Dickens' popular stories which looked as if some pages might be missing, and the third was a dictionary.

"I've looked at them every day, trying to make sense of them," he said. "I've memorized words I know the look and meaning of, like butcher, baker, theatre, inn, and I've tried to find those letters in my books. I've practised writing. Look!"

He looked beneath the box again and pulled out a notebook. He opened a page at random. It was covered in letters and random words which Billy had copied from one of his books, neatly and painstakingly so as to resemble the print on the page.

"Oh, Billy..." Lily felt such a rush of fondness and pity and sympathy that she could scarcely control it. "Of course I'll help you," she said, wondering just how many more lies she was going to have to tell her mother and Harry.

"You *will*?" Billy took hold of both her hands and squeezed them, nearly pulling Lily off her perch on top of the sacks. "Thank you, thank you," he said. "I feel like some music to celebrate."

He picked up his accordion, which was leaning against the wall, and began to play. Halfway through the merry tune, he suddenly burst into song. "Billy, Lily, why are we so silly?" he sang. Then he broke off to say, "Do you know, this is the first time I've realized that our names rhyme! Now, if I called us 'Bill and Lil'..."

He started composing nonsense verses which had Lily nearly crying with laughter. But the last line he sang caused an abrupt change in the atmosphere on the small boat.

"Bill and Lil, they are together still."

He put his accordion gently down on the floor and said, "Do you know, it's almost four years since you first came to hear me sing. I counted the other day."

"I was only twelve then. I was quite small. Then I grew another two inches—"

"And you started putting your hair up. It really suits you when it's all piled up on top. But I like it as it is now, too…"

He leaned forwards and took hold of a strand of Lily's long, unbound hair and moved his hand down so that it streamed through his fingers. "It's so soft," he said. "Like silk."

His hand hovered there, just in front of Lily's left shoulder. Then he touched her arm. She began to tremble violently and her blood was pounding so loudly in her head that she could scarcely hear.

He's going to kiss me, she thought. *At last he's going to kiss me!* Every muscle in her body, every nerve-ending, every fibre, prepared itself to receive the kiss – but it never came. Instead, Billy abruptly lurched to his feet and at the same moment the entire boat seemed to tremble.

Lily felt as if Billy had hit her and knocked the breath out of her. She had been so sure that he was leading up to a kiss that his sudden withdrawal felt like a violent rejection. So when the timbers began to shake and creak around her, she thought that it was her own trembling which was causing the vibration in the boat.

"Tide's coming in," Billy grunted. "You'd better get off the boat. It gets a bit rough when it's straightening up."

As Lily scrambled back down the vertical ladder, the grey waters of the Thames were already lapping at the keel. Twilight had fallen and she was afraid of missing her footing, but she reached the paved Embankment safely, although with very wet feet.

Billy didn't appear to wave her off. She felt like a ghost of the girl who had stepped on to that boat a mere half hour or so earlier. She felt humiliated and tearful. Fancy expecting a boy to kiss you, and then not getting a kiss! Why did the tide have to go and turn just then? If only the movement of the boat hadn't distracted him, he would have kissed her, surely?

Though there was another alternative, that he didn't like her in "that way", and only thought of her as a sister. And yet ... and yet all her instincts told her this wasn't true, that he did like her very much.

But not as much as I like him, she thought ruefully. *I really, really do, and if he doesn't kiss me sometime soon, I shall die!*

"You look cold, dear," her mother said as she came through the door. "You shouldn't have gone out on such a windy afternoon. Come over and stand by the stove, warm yourself up, child. I'll make a fresh pot of tea."

"Where's Father?" Lily enquired, feeling that he might be the one person who could cheer her up right now with one of his dance tunes.

Her mother shrugged. "Fancy asking me where your father is. I'm usually the last person to know anything around here."

Lily wondered if she was included in that remark, but at that moment Archie set up a wail and her mother's concentration was diverted.

That night, everything was blissfully quiet for once as Father and Harry had come in relatively early and sober and, miracle of miracles, Archie was soundly asleep. Yet every time Lily tried to sink into oblivion, she kept hearing Billy's daft song about "Bill and Lil" skipping through her head in a way that was at first vaguely annoying, then infuriating and then, finally, made her cry.

The final stitch of the dress was achieved late on Monday afternoon.

"Shall I take it to Mrs Booth-Edwards for you?" Lily offered, as her mother carefully ironed the newly sewn seams.

"It's very cold tonight. I was thinking of asking Harry to take it, to spare you the long walk. It looks as if it may snow," her mother said. "Look at the sky. The clouds have got that leaden look."

Lily peered out of the window and thought they were more of a sulphurous yellow than a leaden grey.

"I haven't been out of the house all day. I feel stifled in here. Let me take it, Mother, please!"

"Very well," her mother agreed. "But mind you come straight back. You've been out rather a lot lately and I haven't been at all sure where you've been."

Where Lily was going to be between six and six-thirty was outside the Alhambra theatre, snow or no snow!

When she delivered the dress to Brook Street, she was asked to step inside and wait. After a while, Mrs Booth-Edwards herself appeared, beaming with pleasure.

"Capital – just capital!" she boomed. "And exactly the right lace. I knew Cecily could find it if she tried. Please give her this for me, Lily. She handed Lily an envelope which was sealed with sealing wax.

Lily bobbed her a curtsey and thanked her.

"Tell your mother, if you please, that she must come round on Friday morning to discuss plans for a skirt for myself and some dresses for Beatrice." Beatrice was Mrs Booth-Edwards' daughter, who was a year or so older than Lily. "Beatrice will be coming out next year. We have so much to think about. She will need an entire new wardrobe for both the spring and summer seasons. All those Balls…"

Mrs Booth-Edwards gave a dramatic shudder which made her vast bosom quiver. Lily tried not to laugh and gave a smile which she hoped conveyed the fact that she understood Mrs Booth-Edwards' predicament perfectly.

Buoyed up by the successful acceptance of the dress and the promise of further orders for her mother, Lily sang with especial spirit and was rewarded handsomely. She felt like going to look for Billy outside the Oxford, but knew she had better get home. It had started to snow. Her mother had been right.

Cecily Cobbett unsealed the envelope with the aid of a knife and took out the paper money that was inside. There was a note accompanying it.

Dear Mrs Cobbett, it said, in writing as large and over-ornamented as the scribe herself, *I thank you for the dress, which is a perfect fit. I am pleased that you saw fit in the end to provide the lace which I originally requested. You must*

surely agree that it is a great improvement on the inferior lace
which you at first provided. I have no doubt that finding it
must have both inconvenienced you and left you out of pocket,
so I have enclosed an extra nine shillings in recompense.

She looked up from the note, her brow crumpled in puzzlement, and said to Lily, "Nine shillings? That is *most* generous of her. But I don't understand! She bought the lace herself, it was in the parcel when you brought the dress back, you saw it yourself, didn't you?"

"Yes," said Lily, a little sheepishly.

"Is she going mad, do you think?" continued her mother. "Maybe she has reached that age…" She gave a shrug while Lily's mind whirled wildly, trying to find a way out of her dilemma. "I'll have to give her back the money. It wouldn't be fair to keep it," Cecily concluded.

"Of course it would!" Lily protested. "She probably means it as a bonus for getting the dress made so quickly. If you returned it, she would be most offended."

Please do as I say … please, otherwise I shall be in trouble, Lily willed her mother.

But unfortunately, her mother was not on her wavelength that evening. "Imagine what would happen if she remembers buying that lace tomorrow. She'll think I'm a thief, and I'm not having that. Honesty is my middle name and I want everybody to know it," declared Cecily, heroically thrusting the nine shillings back into the envelope.

"Now, find me some paper and a pencil, would you? I need to write her a note. Now don't worry, I'm not asking you to take it all the way back to her, I'll get Harry to take it when he comes in. The sooner this money is out of this house, the better, else it might get spent. I can think of an awful lot of things I could do with nine shillings. I've seen this lovely blouse, Lily, in the palest peach. Three shillings and sixpence, it was... Oh, to have three shillings and sixpence to spend on a new blouse! I can't remember when I last—"

"Mother, you *have* got three shillings and sixpence!" Lily broke in in a quiet but firm voice. She knew she had just cooked her own goose, but it would be worth it to see the look of delight on her mother's face when she realized that the blouse could be hers after all.

"Now, Lily Cobbett, I brought you up to be an honest girl. I can't believe I'm hearing you say that we should keep Mrs Booth-Edwards' money!"

"It *isn't* Mrs Booth-Edwards' money," Lily said, looking her mother squarely in the eye. "It's mine ... or rather, it's yours now. I bought that lace with *my* money – money I've earned."

Her mother's reaction was quite the opposite to what she had anticipated. Instead of smiling in delight and hugging her in gratitude, all the colour drained out of Cecily's face, leaving it paper-white.

"I can't believe a daughter of mine could have sunk to this – to streetwalking!" she said in a strangled voice. "After all I've done for you. I had such high hopes..."

Lily gasped in shock. "Mother, how *could* you think that?" she began, but Cecily waved her hand weakly.

"Leave me," she said. "Go. If you want to be on the streets, then go on them, but don't think you can remain living under this roof. You, of all my daughters ... my favourite..."

Lily's mother burst into tears. As Lily put an arm round

her to comfort her, Cecily shrugged her off. "Go away," she said hoarsely. "Just get out." Picking up the envelope, she flung it towards the door. "Take your tainted money. You'll need it for lodgings," she said.

"Mother, please listen to me. I didn't earn this money the way you think I did. I earned it—"

Cecily raised a tear-ravaged face. "I don't want to hear how you earned it. I just want you out of my sight. Now, *go!*"

Chapter 8

Confused, not knowing what to do, Lily left and closed the door behind her, then collapsed on the landing, sobbing so loudly and heartbrokenly that she didn't hear the tramping of her father's boots as he came up the stairs.

"What-ho!" he called heartily. "Had a tiff, eh? Tell your old papa all about it."

Through her misery, Lily recognized that her father was sober for once. Perhaps it was too early for him to have got rollicking drunk, or maybe he had run out of money. He crouched down to Lily's level and put an arm around her, crooning, "There, there, then."

Lily rested her dark head against her father's ginger one. Nobody had inherited her father's colouring. Her brothers and sisters were all dark, apart from Archie, who still hadn't sprouted a single hair.

"I was only doing my best," Lily gasped through her sobs. "I thought it would help!" She raised huge, drowned grey eyes up to her father's green ones.

Her father rearranged himself into a more comfortable sitting position and pulled Lily onto his lap as if she had been a toddler. "Now, kindly start this story from the beginning so that I can understand," he ordered gently.

"Well, you know how much I like singing? And you know I lost my job at Collyers? I know this boy called Billy who sings outside the Old Mo…"

Lily unfolded her story.

"And Mother thought I had earned the money by working as a … a…" She knew the bad word, "prostitute", but couldn't say it.

"I think I know what you mean." Her father stood up and pulled her to her feet. "We all think you have a very sweet voice, Lily, but singing, that sort of singing especially, is no way for a young lady to earn a living. I understand how you wanted to help us out – it's very generous of you, m'dear, and no more than I would expect from a child of mine, but really, this singing lark has got to end or it'll be the death of your mother. Promise me that you'll never go out singing again!"

Lily gazed at her father and bit her lip. She nodded half-heartily and mumbled, "I promise."

"Louder…" he insisted.

"*I promise!*"

"That's better. Now, let's go in and explain all this to your mother…"

Lily had to repeat the same promise to her mother no fewer than five times before she was satisfied. Then Harry came in and when he heard about the goings-on, he grinned wickedly. "Well, you can't say I spilled the beans, Sis, though I have to admit now that I did know about it. You see, I've seen you." He looked utterly triumphant.

"You never!" Lily gasped. "Where?"

"Outside the Oxford, when I took Dora to a show."

"Oho? So the market are paying you enough to take

young ladies out, are they? When I was your age…"

Lily had no wish to hear her father's reminiscence. This was talk between men. She excused herself and went into the other room, where she splashed cold water over her face from the bowl on the dressing-table and tried to repair the ravages of her crying fit.

She was sitting on the edge of the bed, attempting to read a book by candlelight, when her mother tapped on the door and came in.

"Did you mean it about the blouse?" she said.

Lily gave her a watery smile.

"Thank you, dear, I'll treasure it, but you must have the rest of the money back."

"Nonsense! Put it towards food for us all," insisted Lily.

Her mother hesitated, then took a step towards her and enfolded Lily in her arms. "I'm sorry I was so angry, dear. You know my bad temper!" she apologized. "I do fly off the handle. These headaches don't help…"

"It's all right," said Lily. Her mother seemed in the right mood for her to bring up the burning subject, so she tried. "Mother," she began, "you know we could do with more money and I could earn more than Harry and Father put together if you would only let me go out singing."

"*No!*" Her mother was utterly emphatic. "Never!" she added for emphasis. "I would far rather starve than have you cheapen yourself in that way, acting like a gypsy or a beggarwoman. No, your father and Harry and I will all do our best to find you something. Besides, now that I am getting that big order that Mrs Booth-Edwards mentioned in her letter, I shall need you to help me. If you can learn to do some of the sewing, you will be earning your keep."

"Oh, Mother! You know I can't sew!" Lily protested.

"I think that, with a little effort and concentration..." Lily's concentration left her and she let her mother ramble on, conscious only of the leaden weight in her heart. She couldn't sing... She wasn't to be allowed to experience ever again that wonderful, soaring feeling of having power over an audience... Never again would she hear the applause, hear the chink of coins being thrown her way. *And she wouldn't see Billy!* That was the worst thought of all.

Thanks to Lily's nest-egg, Christmas 1898 was the best Christmas they had ever had. On Christmas Day there was a big stuffed turkey, potatoes and sprouts and plum pudding to follow. Mr Cobbett had begged, borrowed or stolen a bottle of brandy and they all got a bit merry. In fact, it seemed the brandy even penetrated through his mother's milk to Archie, because he was extremely gurgly and good-tempered and slept like a log for two nights running.

On Boxing Day, Millie brought her family to visit. She and her husband Gerald had two-year-old twin girls. The day after that, they went to visit Edie and George. Lily really missed Elizabeth, who had written to say that she was needed by her employers and couldn't get away.

Once the excitement of Christmas and New Year were over, Lily started to fret. The weather was terribly cold – snow winds all the way from Siberia, everybody said. When Lily took the jug down to the milk cart, the milk-man had to chip the milk from his churn and drop it into the jug in frozen chunks. It was said that a cab horse's hooves had frozen to the road and it could only be released after considerable efforts with a burning brand, which set fire to the unfortunate animal's fetlocks.

The Cobbett family were suffering, too. There was little work at the market as much of the produce could not get through since the main routes were blocked by snowfalls. Harry and Father spent more time than usual at the inn and as for Lily, the strain of not seeing Billy, and not being able to sing, made her feel as dull and despondent as a prisoner in a cell.

Then, three weeks into January, her mother's ever-present cough suddenly grew considerably worse and she took to her bed, leaving Lily to look after Archie. Although she took the baby to her mother at feeding times, it seemed the milk she was providing was deficient, because the baby was thin and sickly-looking and, like his mother, grew worse every day.

Father and Harry, spending little time at home, seemed oblivious to the extent of the tragedy unfolding beneath their own roof.

"Oh, it's just a little winter cold," Father said cheerfully, while Mother, not wishing to worry him, nodded her agreement. But Lily could see that it was something far, far worse and one day, when her mother appeared flushed and listless and thrust Archie away from her, she realized that something just had to be done.

She took the fretful baby down to Mrs Molloy, saying, "Please could you look after him? Just for an hour? I must go out on some errands and Mother isn't well."

The fat, motherly woman frowned. "I've heard that cough of hers. Terrible, it is. Tell you what, I'll mix her up some of my potion. You can take it up to her when you come back."

Lily thanked her and made her escape, leaving Mrs Molloy rocking Archie to and fro in her arms in front of a fire that was far hotter than the flickering, spitting one in the grate upstairs.

It was matinée time. Lily would be lucky to find a queue which didn't already have its busker. But she was lucky. The Drury Lane Theatre itself had a queue just begging to be entertained, and Lily set about entertaining it.

That day she happened to be wearing her blue coat with a purplish blue shawl thrown over it, one of her mother's which she had "borrowed". She hadn't worn the coat for some time as it wasn't her warmest, but the colour had appealed to her today and she thought she was unlikely to freeze to death in half an hour. Halfway through a song, she thrust her icy hands into her pockets and the fingertips of her left hand encountered something bristly. When she took it out, she found it to be a sprig of lavender, the stalks bound in blue cotton. She remembered now. She had last worn the coat when visiting her sister Edie. Edie had been making lavender bags and had given Lily some sprigs she had left over. She thought she had put them all in with the bedding, to sweeten and freshen it, but this one had somehow got left behind in her pocket.

She sniffed it, then suddenly the words of an old song came to her. *Lavender Blue...* She sang it, and on an impulse she changed the words to, "When you are king, diddle, diddle, I shall be queen." She smiled as she sang, and she kept the sprig of lavender clasped in her fingers, sniffing it from time to time. It made her think of summer in warmer, sweeter, far-off climes where nobody ever died of cold in winter.

"While you and I, diddle, diddle, keep ourselves warm…"

She didn't realize how much longing she put into those words, or how the expression on her face affected her audience, but several tears were wiped away and the applause was long and the coins generous in amount.

The crowd started filtering into the theatre. Lily gathered up her money, hoping it would be enough to pay for a doctor and for the vital medicine she felt sure both her mother and baby Archie needed. She stood up, about to go, when a man came walking up to her.

"That voice," he said. "I've missed it. I used to hear it coming from a window in Betterton Street but I haven't heard it for a long time. I thought you must have gone away."

Lily gave him a quizzical look. He was well-dressed and in early middle-age, and there was something about him that was ever so slightly familiar.

"My mother is ill, so we have had to keep quiet at home," she explained.

"I'm sorry to hear that." He withdrew a card from a leather folder in the inside pocket of his thick velour overcoat. Lily placed it in her own pocket without looking at it, as it seemed ill-mannered to do so while he was still standing there.

"Have you ever worked inside a theatre, as opposed to outside?" he asked her.

Lily shook her head.

"I think that you could go far with that voice," he said. "What is your name, child?"

"Lily Cobbett," she replied.

"Hmm. We'll have to think of a more attractive name for you than that. Lily is all right, but *Cobbett*…" He took a step back and narrowed his eyes thoughtfully. "Lavender Blue," he said. "How about that? You could wear a pretty lavender dress and that song could be one you open your act with. Not end it, mind – don't want to leave 'em crying. Start them off with a sob in their hearts, then cheer them up with something happy. What do you think?"

Lily had no idea what he was talking about.

"Come and see me one morning, around eleven," he said. "Ask for me at the main door. Don't forget, will you?"

Lily stared at him and nodded, then shook her head. She felt completely confused. Who was he to tell her that there was something wrong with her name and she should change it to Lavender Blue?

He fished in his pocket, withdrew a coin and pressed it into her hand. Then he disappeared into the theatre. Lily noticed how the doormen touched the peaks of their caps as he passed them. He was obviously a man of some importance.

However, she was robbed of a chance to glance at his card by the sudden appearance of a tiny, bearded hunchback.

"Hello, Titch," she greeted him.

"Jago was wondering what happened to you," he said.

She told him about being banned from performing, and handed over the regulation share of the money, completely forgetting about the gentleman's coin, which was sitting next to his card in her pocket.

"If you're starting again, you must come and see Jago or else he will be angry," Titch said warningly.

"That won't be necessary," chimed in another voice and a tall male figure stepped out of the shadows.

"Billy!" cried Lily in delight. "Oh Billy, it's so good to see you. I—"

The eager smile was dashed from her face by the cold look in his eyes. His icicle stare swept her from head to foot, chilling her even more than the east wind that was blowing. Titch, sensing that something private and personal was going on, scuttled off towards the next theatre, while tears sprang to Lily's eyes. Oh, she had missed him so much! Why was he acting this way? Did he think she had been avoiding him deliberately?

"I haven't been allowed out," she explained. "Now Mother and the baby are very sick so I need money for the doctor."

"And you never thought of coming to find me? I could have helped you, Lily. You could have sung with me. But from what I've just overheard, this isn't the first time you've busked on your own."

Lily hung her head. "No," she admitted. "I was hoping you wouldn't find out."

"I never thought we'd end up as..." He hesitated for an instant, then said, "*rivals*," very emphatically.

"But we're not! There are plenty of theatres, there's room for both of us to sing," she pointed out.

"We both do the same sort of material," he said. "And you have the advantage of being a pretty girl."

Normally, being called "pretty" by Billy would have made her glow with pleasure, but the way he had just said it made it sound more like an insult.

Still, she wasn't going to let him win this argument. "What about the songs you write? Nobody else sings those," she said. Then, in an effort to mend things between them, she said, "And I meant it about teaching you to read and write. As soon as the weather and Mother's health improve…"

Billy gave a disbelieving toss of his head. "You never intended wasting your time on someone like me! You were just awaiting your opportunity to get spotted by the likes of James Graydon. You *used* me, Lily!"

Lily hardly heard his last accusation. "Who's James Graydon?" she asked him.

"The man who gave you his card. I saw everything. That's what I meant when I said it wouldn't be necessary for you to have anything to do with Jago any more."

"I really have no idea what you're talking about," Lily said, utterly perplexed.

"James Graydon is the manager of the Old Mo, Lily. And, from the way he was talking, he obviously intends to put you on the stage and turn you into a music-hall star!"

Chapter 9

Without so much as a "goodbye", Billy had walked off down the road, leaving Lily staring at the card which she had taken out of her pocket. Sure enough, it bore the name James Laurie Graydon. What was it he had said? Ask for him any morning?

Too many confused thoughts and feelings were whirling round inside her for her to make an instant decision as to which morning. The most important thing right now was to find a doctor. As for Billy… She shook her head. There would be plenty of time to think about Billy Morgan. For months now, she seemed to have thought of little else.

Mrs Molloy gave her the address of a good chest doctor who lived off Tottenham Court Road. Having looked in on her mother and found her to be no better, Lily ran all the way to the doctor's, arriving dishevelled and panting, her damp hair hanging in long black ropes around her face.

The woman who opened the door to her looked askance at the patched and panting figure. "Yes?" she said curtly.

"Doctor Middleton, please! It's my mother and my baby brother. They—"

"Can you pay? A visit from the doctor costs ten shillings," the woman said, looking at Lily suspiciously.

"I have money," Lily said, drawing herself up to her full height, sweeping her hair back from her face and lifting her chin defiantly. But her heart was thumping. Did she have as much as ten shillings? She stuck her hands in her pockets and clenched them, willing the money to be there, then her fingertips curled around something hard. It was the money the theatre manager had given her. She took it out, glanced at it and realized, from its gleam, that it was not copper but gold! A gold guinea.

The woman saw it, too. "Come in," she said in a kindlier tone, holding the door open for Lily.

The doctor was with a patient and Lily had to wait, but eventually he emerged from his consulting rooms, a big, portly man with a shock of grey curls and a hearty, booming voice. He had a nice smile, though, and Lily felt heartened at the thought of her mother under his care.

She explained their symptoms and he said that he would come at once. On the way up to their dwelling, Lily collected Archie from Mrs Molloy.

"He won't take anything, not even milk," the bulky Irishwoman reported. "I think he's fading away."

A lump formed in Lily's throat as she held out her arms for the baby. The doctor said he would wait until they got upstairs to Lily's own rooms before examining him, and Mrs Molloy gave Lily a pitcher of hot water to take up with her.

As soon as she opened the door, Lily could hear her mother's harsh, rasping breathing. The doctor heard it, too, and went straight into the chilly room where Cecily Cobbett lay. He only had to look at her to pronounce the dreaded word, "Pneumonia."

He took his stethoscope from his black bag. A quick listen to Mrs Cobbett's chest and a few light thumps to her lungs confirmed his opinion.

"You must make this room as warm as you can. Move her by the stove if necessary. She has a high temperature and will be very susceptible to draughts, which could kill her," Dr Middleton said. Lily wished her father had been here, or Harry. What if she didn't remember everything the doctor told her? Then she had the good idea of writing it down.

The doctor said that there would be a "crisis", when the fever would try and burn her up. She had to be kept upright and bent forward, given inhalations of friar's balsam and encouraged to cough up as much as possible of the liquid which was clogging her lungs. The doctor prescribed tablets and herbs, to be obtained from the apothecary, and said that her mother must be encouraged to drink hot beef broth. "She looks half-starved," he said. "Now, let's look at the little chap."

There was nothing wrong with Archie but malnourishment and a winter cold, the doctor said. His mother had no goodness in her milk and a wet-nurse had to be found right away. Fortunately, he knew of a good one in Red Lion Street. She had had six children and her breasts had never stopped producing milk. Lily should take Archie without delay.

"H-how much will she charge?" Lily asked nervously.

When the doctor named the price, Lily knew that her fate was sealed. She must pay James Graydon a visit without delay...

As soon as the doctor had gone, Lily ran to the market

to find Harry, taking Archie with her. Before she left, she had followed the doctor's instructions and had lit the fire in the main room, using the very last of their coal, and persuaded her semi-conscious mother to change beds. She made a pot of tea and left a cup by her mother's bedside, praying that she would drink it. To her knowledge, nothing had passed her mother's lips for two days other than a few sips of water.

She found Harry stationed next to Dora's flower stall. "Please come home, Harry," she begged him. "Mother is very sick and needs these things from the apothecary. I have to take Archie to the wet-nurse, otherwise the doctor says he'll die!"

Tears formed in her eyes and Harry reached out and touched her shoulder in concern. "What doctor?" he asked. "When did Mother see the doctor?"

"I went and got him this morning. Mother was so ill, and Mrs Molloy said that Archie was fading away." The tears spilled out and trickled down her cheeks.

"I suppose the doctor needs paying," Harry said.

The thought that her brother was selfish never crossed Lily's mind. She just replied, "I've paid him," thrust the doctor's prescription into his hand and left, carrying the ominously silent Archie.

That evening was a grim one in the Cobbett household. Without Archie, there should have been silence and peace, but Cecily Cobbett's harsh, painful breathing was audible everywhere. She sounded as if she were drowning.

Messages had been sent to Millie, Edie and even Elizabeth in faraway Shropshire, informing them of their mother's grave illness. Time after time, Harry, Lily or their father would bend the now delirious woman's head over a steaming bowl of mentholated balsam and cover both the bowl and her head with a towel, forming a tent to trap the lung-clearing fumes.

Cecily coughed and thrashed violently around, requiring them to hold her still. In her delirium, she seemed to have the strength of three people. From time to time she called for Archie and started wrenching at her nightgown, trying to feed an invisible baby.

"Ssh now, Mother, ssh!" went Lily, bathing her brow with cool water as the doctor had instructed.

She was no better the next day, but Lily knew she could not delay her audition with James Graydon — not if there were to be more medical bills. So, at eleven, having shooed Harry and their father off to work at six, assuring them that she would remain at her mother's bedside and send for them if there was any change, Lily left her mother in the care of Mrs Molloy and, in her best dress and her mother's black coat, went off to the Old Mo.

At the door, she showed the card Mr Graydon had given her. "He asked me to come," she said.

"Are you after a cleaner's job?" asked the man at the door.

"Certainly not! I'm a singer," Lily informed him proudly.

The man looked surprised, but ushered her to Mr Graydon's office.

"Ah! If it isn't Lavender Blue," he exclaimed. "But you're not in blue today. Why's that?"

"I ... I didn't think," Lily said hesitantly.

"Come along then, come along. Have you got an accompanist? I thought maybe that boy with the accordion... You were singing with him the very first time I ever saw you."

Lily shook her head. "I do sing with him sometimes. I could always go and find him." She gave Mr Graydon a hopeful look. Maybe this was her way of winning Billy back. If only she could get Billy in here, then maybe Mr Graydon would allow him to audition, too, and give him a place on the bill.

"Run along, then," he said. "Try to be back in half an hour as I shall be busy after that."

It was going to take her all of that time to rush down to the boat and fetch Billy. He mightn't even be there. But she wasn't prepared to deprive him of his big chance and, in a fever of excitement, she sped down to the Strand and along the Embankment to Billy's boat.

The tide was high, the boat level with the landing stage. "Billy, Billy! It's me, Lily!" she shouted, rapping on the porthole. There was a stirring inside. A piece of tarpaulin was moved and Billy's face appeared at the glass. The tarpaulin was then replaced, but Billy didn't appear.

"Billy, Billy, it's important!" she yelled, banging even harder on the glass. "Mr Graydon wants to hear you play," she added, thinking that if anything was going to lure him out, that would. But Billy refused to come out and she didn't have time to scramble on to the boat, lift the hatch and try and persuade him.

"If you want to miss the biggest opportunity you've ever had, be it upon your own head!" she hurled at the window, then marched angrily and puzzledly all the way back to Drury Lane.

Surely he should have jumped at the chance to play for Mr Graydon! What was wrong with him? Couldn't he see what a big break she was handing him on a plate? Or perhaps that was what was wrong: that he wanted to make it on his own merit and his pride wouldn't permit him to take up an opportunity which came via her.

Maybe he was ill and that was why he wouldn't come out. Or perhaps he had someone with him and was in the middle of an important conversation. But who could possibly be so important that he wouldn't break off what he was talking about for five minutes in order to discuss his musical future? *Unless he was with a girl...*

Lily stopped dead in her tracks as she conjured up a picture of a girl sitting on that pile of sacking where she had sat, being introduced to the intricacies of Billy's special Eastern tea-boiler. A girl who was getting those kisses that Billy hadn't given to her! Jealousy seethed within her, but she fought it down. Billy Morgan was not worth thinking about. But the music-hall most certainly was!

Mr Graydon was still in his office when she returned.

"Sorry, I couldn't find Billy," she lied. "He's very good, though. You really ought to listen to him sometime." Why was she trying to help him when he hated her? *Really, Lily Cobbett, you can be very stupid!* she chided herself.

"Good buskers are two a penny. You've got something special," he said. "The sooner you're on the stage, the sooner other people can enjoy that exquisite voice of yours." He stood up and opened his office door. "Joe?" he called. A completely bald man of indeterminate age appeared. "Joe, tinkle the ivories for us, would you? I want to hear this young linnet sing."

Lily thought she had never felt lonelier and more scared in her life. There she was, standing on a great big stage in front of rows and rows of empty seats. Mr Graydon spoke to Joe and all of a sudden she heard the familiar tune of *Lavender Blue*. The key was a little low.

"Could you play it higher? Like this?" she called, and began to sing it in her normal key.

The pianist adjusted his fingers accordingly and Lily launched herself into song.

"Again," called Mr Graydon when she had finished. "Sing it the way you did when I heard you the other day. You did it with real feeling then."

Lily screwed up her eyes. She thought of her mother, lying in a freezing bedroom, and Archie, thin and white in the doctor's arms. Then, primed with sadness, she sang again.

"Exquisite," Mr Graydon said. "That really must be your theme song, Lily – I mean, Lavender. We'll dress you in a lavender dress and you can hold a big basket of lavender, and afterwards you can throw sprigs of it to the audience. What else can you sing?"

At first, Lily's mind went blank. Then suddenly one of Billy Morgan's songs popped into her head. "You won't know this one," she told the pianist, and sang it unaccompanied.

To her disappointment, Mr Graydon shook his head. "It's not really Music-Hall, that one," he said. "Too poetic. Try something else."

Half an hour passed, maybe more, with Lily switching from one type of song to another. Cheerful, sad, comic, she sang the lot and at the end, Mr Graydon said, "My first impression still stands. I think you have a rare talent, child. Have you a blue dress?"

"Only my old, patched one," she answered.

"Then wear that for now, so that you look like a waif, a little match girl. We'll try you out on the first house tonight. The second house can get a bit rough and noisy sometimes. You'll be on second to last and after that ... we'll see."

"Will I get paid for it?" Lily asked, agog with excitement.

Graydon laughed. "Of course, my dear. All my artistes get paid, otherwise why would they wish to appear on stage? Now, run along with you. I'll get you added to the playbill. It will only be in small letters because we'll have to squeeze you in, but your name will be there," he assured her.

Lily felt as if she were walking on air as she made her way homewards. Scarcely had she got through the door than she heard Mrs Molloy's voice.

"Lily, oh Lily, thank the Lord you've come. Your mother's worse, I think it's the crisis. I've sent for Doctor Middleton."

Chapter 10

By six o'clock, every member of the Cobbett family, apart from Edward and Elizabeth, was crammed into the two rooms at the top of the house in Betterton Street. Mrs Molloy, who enjoyed a drama, set about making endless pots of tea, though Mr Cobbett was seen to sneak whisky into his.

"When will Elizabeth get our letter? What if she doesn't get here in time? It would break her heart," Millie said anxiously, pulling hairpins out of her bun and stabbing them back in again, as she always did when she was nervous.

"Shut up!" hissed Lily fiercely. "Mother's not going to die. She can't!"

Dr Middleton arrived at last and when he saw Cecily, he shook his head and swore that there was nothing more they could do now except pray to the good Lord. They all joined in to say a prayer around her bed. Charlie Cobbett collapsed in tears at the bedside. Lily had never seen her father in such a state. He must really love Mother, she thought.

Cecily was burning up. "If only her fever would break," said Edie, refusing to relinquish her grip on her mother's hand. "If she could just start sweating, it would bring her temperature down."

On the doctor's instructions, they had heaped every blanket they could find on to their mother's bed, although she kept kicking and hurling them off. Edie had brought a bucketful of coal with her in the hansom cab and the fire was now roaring in the grate. The room was uncomfortably stuffy.

Suddenly, to her horror, Lily remembered that she was supposed to be making her stage début in less than half an hour. Snatching her blue dress from the chest where it was kept, she grabbed her coat from the hook behind the door and barged through her relatives.

"Where are you going?" asked an astonished Millie.

"I ... I have to be somewhere," Lily gabbled and fled down the stairs.

She arrived at the Old Mo all out of breath and told the astonished doorman that she was singing that night. He directed her backstage, to a room where the lesser female entertainers got changed and made-up. A stench of acrid sweat, sweet powder and cheap perfume invaded her nostrils as she pushed the door open. Everyone stared as the shabbily dressed young stranger walked into the room, but Lily had no time for introductions. Forgetting modesty, she scrambled out of her dress and into the old blue one, then picked up a comb which was lying around and tried to tease the knots out of her hair.

"And who might you be?" asked the blonde, ringleted owner of the comb.

"Lily ... Lily Cobbett. They call me Lavender Blue. Mr Graydon's trying me out tonight. I'm on next to last," Lily gasped. Her hands were trembling so much that she dropped the comb.

The woman she had been talking to picked it up and said, in broad cockney, "Lawks, ducks, you're never going on stage looking like that. Stand still, will you?"

In an instant, she'd got Lily's hair straight and was dashing lipstick on her mouth. Lily had never had make-up on her face before. Next thing she knew, the woman had a stick of black stuff in her hand and was rubbing it round Lily's eyes.

"There, that's better, isn't it?" she declared, drawing Lily over to the big mirror in front of them.

Lily was horrified at her reflection. She looked as if someone had picked up a piece of coal and rubbed it on each eye, and her mouth looked as if it were covered in blood. In addition, the woman had painted a red patch on each cheek. Still, if that was the correct look for the music-hall stage, then Lily mustn't argue. She felt sure the woman, who said she was a dancer, must know best.

A man, whom Lily felt sure was wearing hair-dye and make-up, popped his head round the door and called out some names, "Lavender Blue" amongst them.

"Where do I go?" Lily asked the woman.

"Just follow Reggie and the rest," was the vague answer, accompanied by a wave of the hand as the woman concentrated on adjusting the bow in her hair.

Lily tagged herself on to the back of the group who were straggling towards the wings of the stage. Suddenly, a hand seized Lily's arm and dragged her into a corner.

"Take that muck off your face, it looks terrible," ordered a voice. It was James Graydon, and he pulled out his pocket handkerchief and thrust it at her.

"I ... I need a mirror," stammered Lily.

"Here – spit. I'll do it."

Lily spat on to the white linen, hating herself for ruining the pristine material. Graydon scrubbed fiercely at her face, asked her to spit again, and launched a second onslaught.

"Who did this to you?" he demanded.

"Er … a woman with blonde ringlets. Says she's a dancer."

"I know the one. Flora Brock. A bit of a cat, that one. Best to keep out of her way. Now you'll do. There's a ventriloquist's act on now, and then it's you. Just wait for the announcement. And don't be scared. This is a kind house and I'm sure they'll like you. I've asked Joe to play *Polly Perkins of Paddington Green* for your encore. Can you manage that?"

Lily nodded. Her throat felt completely dried up. "Could I have some water?" she asked.

Graydon called a lad and asked him to fetch a glass of water for Miss Lavender Blue. Hearing her stage name pronounced with such importance, Lily felt her courage rise. Miss Lavender Blue was an entirely different person to Miss Lily Cobbett. As she made the transformation from Lily to Lavender, swapping one flower for another, Lily was determined to forget all her troubles during those terrifying, heady moments while she was on stage.

Lavender Blue is a very short song. There are only two verses, so it is up to the singer to rend all he or she can from the meaning of the words – which can be just a simple folk song a lad sings to his love, or, as Lily made it, a song of utter, hopeless longing. After she had sung the verses for the first time, Joe, the pianist, played some variations on the tune while Lily did an impromptu dance and mime of a girl imploring her lover to let her love him and warm him. While she did it, she thought of Billy. Where was he? What was he doing? Did he ever think of her? Would he be proud to see her now?

Then Joe changed key and Lily sang the song again, higher, then once again, lower, so that it ended almost on a sob. When she'd finished, the audience was silent — so silent that Lily thought they must loathe her so much that they weren't even going to acknowledge her. But then one person started to clap, and then another, and she realized that what she'd done was to touch their hearts, so that they were all lost in their own private, thoughtful worlds.

The second song saw her in a different mood, preening and strutting as Polly Perkins. The applause was deafening and people were screaming for another song, but Graydon was standing in the wings, beckoning to her to leave the stage.

"I'm going to move you up the bill. Tomorrow you will be advertised as our new sensation and you'll appear third. Both houses. All right!"

"All right," Lily responded, her eyes sparkling. Then, like a horrible, evil shadow creeping across her vision, she conjured up a picture of her home as she had left it, with her mother desperately ill and all the family clustered solemnly round. Tears filled her grey eyes. "My mother may be dying," she told her new employer. "If she dies tonight, then I shan't be here tomorrow."

Graydon nodded thoughtfully. "I quite understand," he said, "but I beg you to send word to me about her state of health. If you aren't here, then we will have to make an announcement to the audience."

He reached out and touched Lily's hand, gazing straight into her eyes. "I will join you in praying for your dear mother's recovery," he said, and his kindliness and concern nearly had her crying.

Lily was scared to go home – scared of what she might find. If her mother had died in her absence, while she was strutting on stage and glorying in the applause, she would never forgive herself. Creeping like a criminal, she tiptoed into the house and up the stairs. There was some commotion going on, but no sounds of weeping and wailing. Was that a good sign, she wondered?

Pushing open the door, she walked in, and was promptly enthusiastically embraced by her sister Millie. "She's all right – Mother's all right!" she announced. "Look!"

Lily looked – and saw her mother, sitting up and being fed beef broth by Edie. Doctor Middleton was hovering by the door, obviously about to leave.

"Will she recover now?" she asked him.

"She will need a lot of care and nursing for the next few weeks. She has to get rid of that fluid in her lungs, but I have prescribed something which will help her cough it all up. She must be kept warm and fed simple, but nourishing food. Hot milk, chicken broth, meat and potatoes. She's a very lucky woman. But then, I hate to lose a patient."

A cold shudder racked Lily at the thought of how close she had come to losing her mother, but she managed a weak smile as she thanked the doctor.

Not one person asked Lily where she had been, for which she was profoundly grateful.

In fact, over the next few weeks, her secret was known to one person only – Mrs Molloy, who sat with Cecily whilst she was doing her twice nightly turn at the Old Mo.

"Go on, girl, get me a ticket," she kept pleading. "I'd love to see you. Fancy having a music-hall star in my house!"

"I can't get you a ticket at the moment. Who'd look after Mother?" Lily reminded her, promising that as soon as her mother was better and she felt able to tell the family about her new career, Mrs Molloy would be the very first person to receive a free ticket to hear Lavender Blue sing.

Lily felt much more confident now. With her wages, she had bought three new dresses which she kept at the theatre, along with her patched old blue one. She had shoes and shawls, hats and her own make-up, which she used sparingly, ignoring the advice of older women like Flora Brock who, jealous of Lily's fresh young complexion, felt obliged to ruin it with powder and paint.

Every night a basket of lavender would be waiting for her and the highlight of her act was when she sang her trademark song and tossed lavender into the not so sweet-smelling audience. She was beginning to gain her own following. Night after night, she could pick out the same faces in the audience. Bouquets would arrive for her backstage and young men would ask to speak with her, but Lily always sent a message to say she was busy, and then slipped out of the theatre in her "disguise", which was her worn old coat and a scarf over her head.

One young man seemed more ardent than the rest. Handsome, he was, with a fierce moustache and glittering eyes and gleaming dark brown hair. He was always in the same box with a group of raucous male friends, some in military uniform. How he waved and called out when Lily appeared on stage – and how disdainfully she ignored him. Since Billy had rejected her, no man could capture her fancy. She missed Billy dreadfully, far more deeply than she would ever have thought. It had just been a childish infatuation, she told herself stoutly. Now she was much more grown up and next time she fell in love, it would be the real thing.

One day, James Graydon called Lily into his office to discuss her act. "I think it's time for some new songs," he said. "People are getting fed up with Little Polly Perkins, and so am I. Have you any ideas? I have a selection here…"

He produced a sheaf of songs, fresh from the publishers Francis, Day & Hunter in Charing Cross Road. "Now there's one here…" he began, but stopped when he noticed that Lily's eyes had glazed over dreamily.

"Do you remember the accordion player? The one who writes songs?"

"You sang a song of his once and I wasn't very impressed, as I recall."

"Well, he's written lots. He's very good. If I were to bring him here, do you think you could spare the time to listen to some, in case there's one good enough for me to sing?"

Graydon looked at the appeal in Lily's eyes. She was so young, so unspoiled, so talented. If she were sweet on this boy and it would make her happy to sing one of his songs, then why not give her the chance? he thought. Then, if the lad turned out to be a hit songwriter in the future, he, James Graydon, would be known for having launched not just one major new star in the music-hall firmament, but two!

Having gained his approval, Lily went in search of Billy, with a shopping list tucked in her pocket. At least she had a genuine reason to be out and about. Her mother was now well enough to be fretting about Mrs Booth-Edwards' big order for her daughter's dresses having gone to another dressmaker. Since her illness, though, her eyesight seemed to have got worse and she could now scarcely read, let alone thread a needle.

"We'll have to get you some glasses," threatened Lily.

"What nonsense! I can't afford glasses, and even if I could, there are things the house needs more," Cecily insisted.

Lily thought of her hoard, now almost too big to fit in its hiding-place beneath the floorboards. She would soon have to think about opening an account at the bank. And maybe next year – oh, sublime thought! – the Cobbetts could buy their own little house, their very own, with a garden and a lavatory and even gas lighting, which would be so much better for Mother's eyes than dim oil lamps and flickering candles.

It was so long since Lily had last seen Billy that she no longer knew where to look for him. She had been to the boat several times but it seemed empty, deserted even. All she knew was that he was never at any of the theatres in or near Drury Lane. She certainly couldn't ask Jago for he would be furious about her having swapped her busking, which was lucrative for him, for the real stage.

Yet it was Jago who solved the problem for her. By the

time she saw his familiar stocky figure approaching her in Tottenham Court Road, his lilac waistcoat was almost level with her lavender coat.

"Hello, Missy. Remember me?" he said sternly. Then, just as she was quailing and wondering which shop she could dodge into, his gruff countenance cracked and he started to laugh.

"Congratulations!" he said. "I hear you're a star now. I always thought you were too good for mere busking."

"Thank you," said Lily, astonished by his reaction. Maybe she had misjudged him, she thought.

"Look out for me in the audience. I shall be there one of these nights," he promised. Then, with a touch of his grey bowler hat, which sported a lilac ribbon to match his waistcoat, he started on his way, until Lily, suddenly remembering her mission, called him back.

"Jago? Any news of Billy Morgan?" she enquired.

"Billy … yes. He went back to Wales. His grandmother died."

"Oh, I'm sorry to hear that," Lily said. "Will he be coming back, do you know?"

"Any time now, I think. We've been keeping an eye on the boat for him and I have his accordion at home, in safe-keeping. He left two weeks ago and said he would be back by the end of February."

It was the 25th now. Lily had a pencil with her, which she had been intending to use to tick off the items on her shopping list. "Please, Jago, have you any paper?" she asked him.

He took out the famous notebook and ripped out a page.

"I'm writing Billy a note. It's really important. Mr Graydon has agreed to hear his songs. He wants a new one for me to sing," Lily said. "You will give it to him as soon as you see him, *promise?*"

Jago Jagger promised solemnly and let Lily use his broad back as a firm surface for her writing. When she'd finished and folded the paper, he promised yet again to give it to Billy – "Even though it might mean my losing yet another source of income," he grumbled.

Four nights later, Lily had just come off stage after finishing her act when Reggie, the man with the dyed hair whose job it was to fetch all the acts when they were due on stage, came to tell her that there were two gentlemen to see her.

Lily made her normal dismissive reply, but Reggie was insistent. "One says he knows you want to see him because you sent him a note. He mentioned someone called Jago," Reggie said.

"Billy! Show him in!" Lily cried delightedly.

Seconds later, a paler, thinner looking Billy nervously opened the door to her tiny dressing-room. "Come in!" Lily said, holding out her arms in welcome. Billy was halfway through the door, his eyes roving the room, taking in the dresses, the hats, the music, the sight of Lily herself in her splendid new gown of ruby satin, when he was abruptly sent staggering by another man who pushed him aside and hurled himself towards Lily with the force of a galloping horse. Above the giant bouquet of pink roses which he thrust at her, she just had time to spot shining dark eyes and a virile moustache before she was caught up in an ardent embrace.

"At last, my dearest darling, at last!" the man cried.

By the time Lily had fought her way out of his clutches, Billy had gone.

Chapter 11

"Who are you?" she asked.

"The name's Ned Gates, Cavalry Sergeant Ned Gates, at your service." He clicked his heels and bowed.

Although she was upset that Billy had seen fit to disappear without staying to find out what was really going on, Lily couldn't help but be impressed. This well-groomed man in front of her seemed to radiate health and vitality. His smile was infectious. Lily smiled back and offered him her hand. "Pleased to meet you, Sergeant Gates."

"Call me Ned," he insisted, bending over her hand and dropping a soft kiss on the back of it. Then he turned her hand over and kissed the palm and each fingertip.

Shocked, Lily snatched her hand away. He was taking liberties that she couldn't allow. But his kisses had felt nice, if somewhat tickly.

He laughed. "I hope you like the flowers," he said. "I've sent you flowers every day since I first saw you, but you would never allow me to meet you. Why was that?"

"Well, I –" Lily didn't know what to say. She wasn't like the other female singers and dancers. She wasn't used to attention from men. "I live just round the corner. My mother is ill and I go straight home after every show. I'm only sixteen," she explained, unaware of how charming her words sounded.

Ned Gates was captivated. "Then please allow me to escort you to your door," he offered. "I'll make sure nobody bothers you or follows you, like that scruffy looking chap who was trying to come in at the same time as me. I'm glad I was there to see him off!"

Lily pursed her lips. She didn't like the idea of Billy being "seen off" and she fully intended to try and find him again and give him the chance he deserved. "That 'scruffy looking chap' was Billy Morgan, a good friend of mine," she told Ned, rather curtly. "He's a singer, too and he writes excellent songs. I asked him to come here and bring me his latest compositions. So I'm afraid you misjudged the situation, Sergeant Gates."

"Ned," he reminded her. "Oh dear." He looked thoughtful. Then he ventured, "Are you … he…?"

Lily pretended not to know what he was talking about. "I must get back to my mother. She is recovering from pneumonia," she said.

Ned seized her hand again. "I didn't mean to upset you. Oh, what a thing to happen on our first meeting. I'm so sorry. I shall go away and never return," he declared dramatically.

He made for the door, but Lily called him back. "Don't go," she said. She had never known anyone quite like him, who did and said things with such a flourish. "You offered to escort me home and I am pleased to accept."

He offered her his arm and she tucked her hand boldly through it and together they sailed through the door, Lily revelling in the looks she was getting. Some of the other girls looked wildly jealous that she had snared such a dashing beau.

When they reached her door, Lily apologized for not being able to invite him in.

"I quite understand," he said. "I shall be in the audience for both houses tomorrow and shall call on you again after the second house, if you permit me."

Lily had never known such perfect manners. "I shall be pleased to see you tomorrow," she informed him.

And indeed she was. Despite the cold and darkness, she agreed to a short walk, just up Parker Street to Kingsway, then along to New Oxford Street and back down Monmouth Street to Drury Lane again. As they walked, Ned told Lily about himself. He was twenty-four and had one brother and two sisters. He came from Kingston-Upon-Thames. His father was a businessman with interests in shipping and wine-importing.

"Father wanted me to join him in the family business but I could never be happy sitting at a desk all day. I like action and travel. I'm a good rider and I can't wait for a nice little war to break out somewhere," he said.

Lily gave a shudder, which she hoped he wouldn't notice, but he did. "Cold, my dear?" he asked. He removed his blue cloak and draped it gallantly round her shoulders. "May I ask you a question of a somewhat personal nature?" he enquired.

Lily's eyes grew round with surprise, but she nodded, intrigued.

"Have you ever walked out with anybody?"

"Of course not! I told you I was only sixteen, and it's true. I shan't be seventeen until the twenty-fifth of May."

"What a coincidence! I shall be twenty-five on the 31st of May. That's very close. Maybe we're very alike!" he declared.

Lily laughed. "We're both Geminis. Did you know that Gemini is the sign of the twins?" she asked him.

"Gemini? What's that? No, I didn't know," he said, sounding slightly affronted, as if fearing that Lily was making fun of him.

Lily rejoiced in the chance to teach him something. "It's our astrological symbol," she said. "Our birthdays take place in the sign of Gemini, the twins. That means we are talkative –"

"I am, that!" affirmed Ned.

" – lively, good at writing and often at music—"

"Did I tell you I can sing?"

"No, you didn't," said Lily.

"I've often sung in the officers' mess and at private parties. I love Italian opera."

Lily looked at him blankly. She knew nothing about opera.

"Do you like Puccini? Ah, *Madame Butterfly*! Sublime, completely sublime. And *La Bohème*..."

"What's a '*bohème*'?" asked Lily.

Ned gave a burst of incredulous laughter. "A Bohemian. From Bohemia. Do you know where Bohemia is?" He proceeded to educate her about Geography and about Puccini, until they suddenly arrived outside her house. As they were standing there, with Ned still in full flow about Italian music, the door burst open and there stood Lily's father.

"What time do you call this, young lady?" he shouted,

his face like thunder. "I'm Lily's father. And who, young man, might you be?"

"Lily... so your real name is Lily. What a truly pretty name," Ned sighed.

"You don't even know her name, yet here she is wearing your cloak? What *is* going on?" demanded Mr Cobbett.

Ned gave a spectacular bow and Lily could see that her father was impressed. "Sergeant Ned Gates, Third Cavalry," he explained. "Pleased to meet you." He seized Mr Cobbett's hand and pumped it energetically. "I have just escorted your daughter, the lovely Lavender Blue, back from her performance at the Old Mo. With her permission, of course. You really should have been there tonight, sir. Her second performance was even better than her first. Entrancing!"

Lily's father looked utterly perplexed. "Lavender Blue? Performance at the Old Mo? Lily, would you kindly explain what's going on?"

Lily felt rooted to the spot with guilt. She gazed anguishedly at Ned. "I ... I hadn't told my family about my singing," she said sheepishly.

"And if I hadn't decided to keep your mother company tonight and come back to find her in the care of Mrs Molloy, we might never have known," Mr Cobbett riposted furiously.

He seized Lily's arm. "Come indoors this minute!" he raged. "Goodnight, young man!"

All Lily could do was give Ned a farewell glance of apology as her father kicked the door shut in his face.

"This is a fine carry-on, I must say!" he fumed, hauling the unwilling Lily up the steep stairs. "We, your parents, should be the first to be informed of own daughter's activities and instead we're the last. Wait till your mother hears about it!"

"I was going to tell her – I was going to tell you both! – but I wanted to wait until Mother was stronger," Lily explained. "Ouch! Father, you're hurting me!"

"Sorry," her father apologized, slackening his bruising grip on Lily's wrist. "You can't blame me for being angry, though. You promised us you'd give up this singing lark and now I find out you've been lying!"

"But I only did it for Mother … for us," Lily sobbed.

"Did what?" Lily's mother was standing in the doorway, holding on to it as she was still very weak. Her voice was quiet, but colder than Lily had ever heard it.

"I found her with a young man – a soldier," Lily's father said.

"I wasn't 'with' him, he was just walking me back from the theatre to make sure I was safe. There are a lot of thieves and vagabonds around on these dark nights," Lily said in her defence.

"You mean to tell me that you've been visiting theatres? Where did you get the money to do that?" Cecily Cobbett asked suspiciously.

"Not visiting them, *singing* in them," said Charlie. "This daughter of ours has been appearing in the music-hall, calling herself Lavender Blue, after she made us that solemn promise never to go out singing again. What do you think of that, Mother?"

"I promised never to go out busking. I didn't say anything about singing properly, as a job," Lily protested.

"Silence, child! Speak when you're spoken to!" her father thundered.

Lily fell into a mutinous silence, though she continued her defiant glare. This simply wasn't fair. Who would have paid for Dr Middleton if she hadn't been able to do so? Her mother might well have died if it hadn't been for Lily's singing, yet they weren't giving her a chance to explain!

"Lily Cobbett, you are a liar and an undutiful daughter. I am deeply disappointed in you. We both are," said her father.

Lily's eyes flashed and her mother gave her a warning look.

"From now on, you are confined to this house, unless accompanied. Is that clear? And as for your soldier laddie, he cannot be a man of honour if he is not prepared to call on us and introduce himself and gain our permission before escorting our daughter."

"But Father, it wasn't like that! And I—"

"Silence! Who gave you permission to speak?"

At that moment, several sets of heavy footsteps could be heard stamping up the uncarpeted stairs to their door.

"Will you answer and send them away please, Cecily? I'm in no mood to talk to anybody," grunted Mr Cobbett.

The next minute, their rooms were invaded by booming male voices and hearty laughter. "Why, Harry! What are you doing bringing Gerald and George to see us? What a lovely surprise!"

George, Edie's husband, swept his mother-in-law towards him and gave her such a smacking kiss that she blushed crimson. Then Gerald, Millie's husband, followed suit, leaving Cecily with one hand on the wall, laughing and propping herself up.

"It's George's birthday –"

"Oh, happy birthday, George!" said Cecily.

" – and we've had a little outing planned for some time," Harry continued. "Decided we'd dine together then go to the theatre. And guess who was the star of the show?"

"Thought he'd arranged it specially for me!" interrupted a rather drunken George.

"Your little sister here!" boomed Gerald, clapping Harry on the back. "How have you kept such a star hidden from the family? She deserves to have her name in lights all over London. All the gents in the audience fell totally in love with her."

"Yes, we met one of them this evening," muttered Lily's father.

"Congratulations, Lily, you're wonderful!" cried George, grabbing her and almost squeezing the life out of her.

"Yes, Sis, you were capital!" agreed Harry. "Completely excellent. Why did you never tell us?"

Lily looked from one parent to the other. "Because..." She left the rest unsaid.

"I bet it was you who paid the doctor!" her father said suddenly. "And I went and thanked Gerald for it!"

Lily stared modestly at her feet. "I told everybody not to say it was me," she mumbled.

"Lily..." Her mother spoke more gently now. "I know you broke your promise, but I thank you," she said and, stepping towards Lily, she put her arms round her and kissed her brow. "Don't be too hard on her, Charlie," she said. "I might not be here now if it wasn't for Lily. And Archie...?" she went on.

"Yes, I have been paying for the wet-nurse, too," Lily confessed.

"Thank you," Cecily said again. "Charlie says that he's thriving."

"Yes, I went to see him yesterday evening. He's a really big boy now," his father said proudly. Lily felt guilty. It was two weeks since she had visited the wet-nurse and seen her baby brother.

"I'm feeling stronger now. I think that tomorrow, if it's not too cold, I would like to visit him myself. Would you walk with me, Lily?"

Lily smiled delightedly. "Of course I will!" she said.

Her mother gave a radiant smile. "I didn't miss him while I was so ill, but I do now, and I long to have him back," she said. "And as for your singing, Lily—"

"Lavender Blue, she calls herself. Lavender Blue, indeed!" scoffed her father.

"Very pretty name. She sings the song and wears a – hic! – blue dress," Gerald butted in.

"I think I would like to go and hear her for myself," said her mother. "Charlie, would you take me to the Old Mo?"

"Oh please, not yet!" Lily begged. "Because I'm new, I'm only doing two songs, but Mr Graydon has asked me to do some new ones. Just give me a couple more weeks and then I should have a proper act worked out. I'm only third on the bill, so far!"

If only she had a brand new, sparkling song of Billy's, she might get to be top, she thought regretfully. She would send him another note, she decided; give him one more chance to share in her good fortune. And if he failed to respond this time, then there was nothing more she could do. Billy Morgan would have to become part of her past.

*   *   *

Next morning, leaning on her daughter's arm, Cecily walked slowly all the way to Red Lion Street to visit her baby son.

"Look, Mother, look! He's got a ginger curl!" Lily shrieked, as the wet-nurse handed Archie to his mother.

Cecily looked at her baby's large dome. "So he has!" she exclaimed in astonishment. "I do declare it's the same colour as your father's. The only one in the family to take after him. Charlie will be so pleased."

Archie, from being a thin, pale little mite of eight months old, was now more than nine months and so fat that Lily thought her arms were going to break as she held him. His face was pink and glowing and his eyes were turning as green as his father's.

"Gug-gug-gug," he burbled, tweaking a strand of Lily's hair. On an impulse she kissed his plump cheek. "Oh Archie… What a beautiful baby brother I've got," she crooned.

"He's been taking broth. I think he can be weaned soon," the wet-nurse told them. "Isn't he a treasure?"

Lily fished in her purse and took out a more generous amount of money than was strictly necessary. The wet-nurse's eyes gleamed in anticipation as she saw it. Lily handed it over, saying, "Thank you for saving my baby brother."

"I'll miss him," the woman said. "He's a real little character. Do bring him back to see me sometime."

Lily carried Archie back inside her coat, with the lower buttons done up to provide some support for his great weight. Her mother talked animatedly throughout the walk. "Tell me all about the theatre. What is it like?" she asked. When Lily had finished telling her, carefully omitting the ruder aspects of backstage life, she started a new topic. "Now tell me all about this soldier boy. Is he your beau?"

Lily blushed and disguised it by nuzzling Archie's curl. "Ned and I have only just met," she said. "He's hardly my beau yet!"

"Good," her mother replied. "For if he were a decent young man with serious intentions, he would have introduced himself to us and asked our permission to walk our daughter home."

"But he couldn't, Mother. You didn't know I was working at the Old Mo. If he'd asked you, you would have found out!"

"Yes, I see," her mother replied. "But you like him, I can tell. I'm not sure if I want you to be courted by a soldier. Soldiers are notoriously fickle. But, as he has a very good background, I'm willing to concede that this particular soldier might be different. I should like to meet him. Could you ask him in tonight, after he's walked you home? That is, if he doesn't mind visiting a slum after his grand house in Kingston..."

From the description he had given her, Ned's house did sound grand. But Lily wasn't deterred by Ned's possible reaction to their circumstances. "If he is fool enough to judge people by where they live, then he is too much of a fool for me," she declared.

"It's getting warmer," her mother observed as they reached the front door, pausing with one foot on the step. "It will soon be spring. Listen! Isn't that a blackbird?"

They both listened intently, until the bird, perched on a chimney-pot, repeated its song.

"It's calling for a mate," said Lily's mother, then burst

out laughing at her daring remark.

Lily joined in. Even Archie gave a gurgle which sounded like a laugh. Lily hadn't felt so happy in ages. The only cloud in the clear blue sky of her mind was Billy Morgan. What had happened to him? Why hadn't he come back to the theatre? He couldn't be that concerned about becoming rich and famous, or he would certainly have made another attempt. Well, she had created the opportunity for him and it was his loss if he didn't take advantage of it. What else could she do?

As for the idea that he hadn't come back because he was jealous of Ned – well, that was patently absurd. Billy had never once thought of Lily in that way. As a friend, yes, but nothing more. If he had been in love with her at all, he would have kissed her that afternoon on the boat. He wasn't a shy boy. There was only one reason for him not to kiss her, and that was because he didn't want to. But she had a strong, thrilling feeling that Sergeant Ned Gates did!

Chapter 12

"What have you told them about me?" Ned demanded as he and Lily drew close to the Cobbetts' house. Three weeks had passed since that first evening when he had walked her home, but Ned had had to spend a week of that away on regimental business. But in those two weeks, she had become quite captivated by him. He was lively, handsome, charming and very solicitous in his attentions to her. And he let her know, in no uncertain terms, that he found her very pretty and that he was a slave to her wondrous voice. What a difference to Billy's lack of interest! At last, Lily felt appreciated by a man other than a member of her family.

"Only that you're a soldier and your family comes from Kingston-Upon-Thames," she told him now.

"What's your brother's name again?" Ned asked nervously.

"Harry." Lily laughed. "You don't have to worry about him, he's only eighteen," she said.

"All the same, I want him to like me."

Lily wrinkled her brow and stared quizzically at Ned. Why did it matter whether or not her brother liked him? Unless, of course, he had had some previous experience in which another girl's brother hadn't!

"Ned, there's something I must ask you," Lily said. "Have you had many lady friends? And have you ever been engaged?"

Ned threw back his head and gave a bark of laughter. "Engaged? I should think not! I'm much too young and busy for that."

"*Busy?*" Lily was flirting, she knew she was.

Ned had the grace to look abashed. "I don't mean busy with affairs of the heart! I mean, with my duties to my regiment."

"You mean, going out drinking and gambling and who knows what else, with those high-living friends of yours?" Lily challenged lightly. She was probing, to find out more about him, in particular to see if he was anything like those friends of his appeared to be – noisy, free-spending, carousing. She didn't think he was. He seemed too sincere and quite serious, when he was with her, at least.

"It's the 'what else' that you really want to find out about, isn't it?" he teased her. "What did you imagine me getting up to?"

"Well ... riding in Hyde Park with titled young ladies. Going to the opera with them."

Ned laughed loudly. "You sweet little innocent!" he said, chucking her under the chin, then tweaking the feather in her new velvet hat, of the deepest midnight blue. "Of course I have taken young ladies riding. And to the opera. But not without their chaperones. Dear me! What sort of a vagabond do you think I am?"

Lily blushed becomingly. They were at her door now. Lily let herself in with the key that hung on a string from the inside of the letterbox. "Come up," she invited. "I'm afraid it won't be what you're used to. Welcome to poverty street!"

"Not for much longer, if your popularity continues to grow," Ned pointed out. Lily had already told him of her dream to buy the Cobbetts their own house. "Why don't you come and live in Kingston? It's a lovely place."

"I'm sure it is, but how would I get to the Old Mo from there?" Lily pointed out.

"Buy a little house in Mayfair and – oh, good evening, Mr Cobbett... Mrs Cobbett." Ned bowed low over Cecily's hand and her eyes met Lily's in a glow of approval. "And you must be Lily's brother, Harry. I'm very pleased to meet you all."

Ned was given the best armchair. For once, the room resembled a living-room, the bed having been dragged into the kitchen and propped against the wall. Lily's mother had worked wonders, covering the battered old table with a beautiful length of golden velvet cloth to which she had spent the afternoon sewing a fringe. A dusty aspidistra, borrowed from Mrs Molloy, stood on the tallboy in the corner, its leaves brushing the ceiling. A blue and red Chinese vase had been dragged from obscurity at the back of a cupboard and given pride of place on the velvet. A bronze candelabrum, a wedding present which had lived in the cupboard next to the vase, stood on the mantel and sent soft candlelight dancing around the walls.

"Charming," Ned complimented Cecily, accepting a glass of port from Charlie. Harry had one, too, but Lily and her mother drank ginger cordial.

Lily's father encouraged Ned to talk about his family, which he was pleased to do. From this, Lily learned that he had no fewer than seven nieces and nephews, and that one of his sisters was married to a titled gentleman with land in Warwickshire. She could see that her parents were impressed.

"Do you think you'll stay in the cavalry all your life?" Charlie asked.

Ned looked somewhat surprised. "But of course!" he exclaimed. "I wish to work my way up the ranks, get as high as I can. I'd like a position of command in India. I've always fancied India…"

A thrill ran through Lily's veins. India! Instantly, her mind became full of the cries of strange birds and she could see a burning blue sky, vivid tropical flowers and feel a hot breeze on her skin. Oh, if only Ned could take her with him!

Cecily wanted to know more about how her daughter looked and sounded on the stage every night. Lily blushed and hung her head in embarrassment as Ned went into rhapsodies about her.

"When can we come and see you, Lily?" her mother begged.

"How about my birthday?" Lily suggested.

"But that's more than six weeks away!" protested her mother.

"It will take me all of six weeks to perfect my new act," Lily said. "I haven't even found the right songs yet."

No sooner had she said that than a dark shadow appeared to come into the room, causing the lights to dim as if the wing of a great black bird had swept between her and the oil lamp on the dresser. At first, she couldn't think what had caused the feeling. Then she realized it was the thought of Billy Morgan – though why thoughts of him should affect her deeply enough to dampen her spirits at an important moment like this, she had no idea.

She made an effort and pushed away the picture of Billy's face which had formed in her mind's eye. *Go away, Billy,* she thought savagely. *You have no right to be intruding into this room, spoiling everything. You don't love me, you don't even like me, so get out of my mind!*

"Lily? Are you all right, dear? You are looking a little peculiar," her mother asked anxiously.

Lily shot her a radiant smile. "I'm quite all right, Mama," she replied.

"Mama, indeed! So posh!" Cecily gave a genteel little laugh. "Mama" was how Ned referred to his mother.

After an hour or so, Ned got to his feet and announced that he had better be going.

"Oh, let me show you out," Lily said eagerly, encountering a raised eyebrow from her mother, who warned her, "Come straight back up, won't you? No wandering off into the night. I know what you're like for walking, Lily Cobbett. As bad as your father!"

Lily shushed Ned on the staircase, for fear of waking their neighbours in the other rooms. She opened the front door quietly, but not so quietly as to deter Mrs Molloy from pushing a determined nose round her door, to see who was coming and going in her house.

The night air was no longer freezing. It was a pleasure to stand for a few moments on the step without shivering.

"Thank you for coming," Lily said to Ned. "It wasn't too bad, I hope?"

"Not at all! I enjoyed meeting your family," Ned said. "Your father's a real character."

"I hope you can meet the others someday. Edie and Millie often visit, though we haven't seen Edward for two years. He—"

Lily's words ceased as she was suddenly trapped by Ned's arms and being crushed against him so hard that she could feel the metal buttons of his jacket through her dress. She felt his moustache tickle her forehead, then he released one arm from its powerful grip around her and raised her chin so that her face was tilted up to his.

"Sweet Lily…" His mahogany eyes smouldered into hers. She felt herself quivering with excitement – and then his lips came crushing down on hers, claiming them so powerfully that when he released her, she was panting and could hardly stand up.

"Good-night, sweetheart," he said. "*May* I call you that?"

Lily didn't know what to say, so she nodded.

"Just mine? No one else's?"

She nodded again. Ned smiled a proud, triumphant smile, blew her a kiss, then went striding down the road. But at the corner he turned, looked back and blew her another kiss, which Lily returned before dashing through the door and up the stairs into the safety of those familiar rooms.

Chapter 13

Two mornings later, on a Thursday, Lily left the house determined to find Billy. She had to have some songs to show Mr Graydon, otherwise, as she was his special protégée, he would insist on her singing a song of his own choosing.

She went down to the boat but there was no response to her knockings and callings, so she walked back up to the Strand. Jago was at his usual window seat, reading his usual copy of *The Times* and smoking an odiferous Russian cigarette. Lily handed him the note for Billy which she had written in advance, suspecting that he might try to avoid her. Jago promised to read it to him as soon as he saw him.

Please, Billy, I must have those songs right away, she begged. *None of the songs that have been suggested to me are nearly as good as yours. But none of your political ones, please. A love song would be best. What about that one you used to sing, about the Welsh girl on the farm? That was very nice, and had a good melody. If you come, I can write down the words. Ever your friend. Lily.*

Then, on an impulse, Lily issued an invitation. "My family and friends are all going to come to the theatre on my birthday, the twenty-fifth of May, to hear me sing. I would love it if you came, too," she said.

Jago beamed at her. "I would love to, but are you sure you don't mind introducing your parents to a character like me?"

"What's wrong with you?" Lily laughed. "Any friend of mine is a friend of theirs. They'll love you, especially when I tell them that you started off my singing career."

"Ten per cent?" Jago said, his eyes glinting mischievously.

Lily pulled a face. "I give every penny to my mother. You wouldn't deprive a poor, starving mother with a sick baby to feed, now would you?" Archie was hardly sick any more, but she knew she had painted a pathetic picture.

"Get along with you!" Jago chuckled. "I shall do my best to join your party on May the twenty-fifth."

"Make sure you're there – and Mrs Jagger, if you'd like to bring her," said Lily. "And do please try to find Billy for me…"

Having kissed her once, Ned Gates started to make a habit of it, and Lily had absolutely no objection. *Oh, how lucky I am to have met him now, at the end of winter, instead of at the beginning,* she thought happily. Now the night winds were getting warmer and the sunshine stronger and they didn't need a fire at home every day. The windows could be unsealed and opened to freshen the rooms. Washing could be hung out again, to flap dry in a strong breeze. Baby sparrows squeaked from a nest just above the kitchen window. Lily once tried to count how many times the parents flew back and forth with morsels for their brood, and had to give up.

Ned wasn't able to come to the theatre or meet her every

single night. Sometimes he paid visits home, or had things to do connected to his regiment. On those occasions, Lily found herself missing the excitement of their walks and talks – and dearly missing those passionate, bruising kisses which were such proof of his powerful love for her.

Four days following her delivery of the note to Jago, Billy Morgan still hadn't bothered to come to the theatre, so Lily, with the help of Joe, the pianist, set about learning two from the sheaf of songs James Graydon had provided. One was called *The Nightingale*, and allowed Lily a chance to demonstrate her top notes as she emulated the bird's warble. The other was a song about a lass in love with a sailor. He had gone to Amsterdam and she voiced her fears about all the temptations that port might put his way. It made her wonder about her brother Edward. They had received a postcard recently which had come all the way from Venezuela, in which he reported that he had acquired a parrot, like a typical sailor. Lily wished he would come home.

On the morning of the fifth day, she was rehearsing her new repertoire with Joe when she sensed, rather than saw, someone slip into a seat in the dark auditorium. She could feel eyes upon her and it caused her to fumble with her lyric sheets and drop them and miss a top note, which came out as cracked kind of cough.

"Stop please, Joe," she asked him. Then she saw a hump-backed figure detach itself from the shadows and walk down the centre aisle towards her. The hump detached itself and changed into the shape of an accordion.

"Billy!" she cried and raced for the steps. She ran along the front of the orchestra pit and came to a halt in front of him. "I'm so glad you're here!" she told him, feeling her smile take over her face.

But Billy didn't smile back, which caused Lily's own delighted smile to die on her lips. "You asked me for some songs," he said curtly, and began to play.

"Not here. Up on the stage," Lily insisted, grabbing his elbow.

Billy followed unwillingly. He climbed on to the stage and stood at one side, resisting Lily's attempts to persuade him to stand in the centre.

"Joe, fetch Mr Graydon quickly, please!" she called urgently. "He must hear these songs."

When Joe had gone, Lily suddenly felt awkward. Why was Billy so silent? Why wouldn't he chatter to her like he normally did? Or was he waiting for her to apologize for Ned's behaviour? She decided that must be the case.

"That night you came to the dressing-room—" she began.

Billy cut her short with an angry gesture. "It doesn't matter," he said.

"But it does!" Lily protested. "It's spoilt our friendship."

"Friendship? Pah!" Billy made a spitting sound. "So that's what you thought it was!"

What does he mean? Lily thought. *What else could it have been? We were friends for a long time, even if a few months ago, before I met Ned, I'd have liked it to be something more. It's jealousy making him like this. He's jealous of my success and too proud to accept my help, so I've got to help him get over it.*

"Well, hello at last, young man. Let's hear your songs," James Graydon called from the auditorium. He sat down in a front row seat and folded his arms expectantly.

"There are only two I want you to hear," Billy said.

"Only two? But you must have written hundreds!" protested Lily. "He has, Mr Graydon. He composes all the time."

"Only two," insisted Billy. Lily was furious with him. How dare he act so churlishly — and in front of James Graydon, too! Didn't he realize what Mr Graydon was capable of doing for him, if he liked him?

Billy commenced playing. The first was the song she knew, the one about the Welsh girl. He had made some improvements to it and added another couple of verses.

"Yes, a nice song. Very nice," Mr Graydon said. "What else have you got for me?"

"I hope you won't mind, but before I sing my brand-new one, I'd like to sing you some extra verses which I wrote for *Lavender Blue*. I know it's a traditional song and shouldn't be altered, but it's Lily's theme song and it's only short, so I thought..."

"Let's hear it, then," Mr Graydon encouraged him.

Billy sang the new verses.

"We have no fire, diddle, diddle,
  What shall we do?
But you have me, diddle, diddle,
  And I have you.

Lie in my arms, diddle, diddle,
  While the wind blows.
Don't mind the rains, diddle, diddle,
  Don't mind the snows.

*   *   *

Don't mind the fog, diddle, diddle,
Don't mind the storm.
Whilst you and I, diddle, diddle,
Keep ourselves warm."

With Billy's additions, a song about poor people dreaming about how their lives would be improved if they were king and queen, had become a song about two lovers. Lily thought it was a bit too obvious and spoiled the innocent appeal of the song.

Billy looked at her and, getting no reaction, shrugged and started to play again. He sang a song about two children, a boy and a girl, playing with a toy boat. Then the boy starts wishing he was grown-up.

"If my tiny boat could float
Across the ocean wide.
Taking us two side by side,
You would make a lovely bride…"

Lily felt her cheeks growing pink as Billy sang it. She was thinking about Ned. But then she started thinking about her big brother, Edward. He actually was floating across the ocean in a boat. Had Billy been thinking about him when he wrote the song?

"We would sail my ship of love
For ever and a day.
I hope no wicked pirate comes
And steals my boat away."

*   *   *

The song was called *Ship of Love*. In subsequent verses, the boy and girl grew up, became engaged, then the girl eloped with a sailor. The young man was left alone. He found his old toy boat and sang the wistful song to it.

Lily found she had a lump in her throat when the song finished. Mr Graydon was absolutely silent, he didn't even clap. Then, as all three stood mutely looking at each other, wondering who would venture to speak first, James Graydon swallowed and said, somewhat hoarsely, "That's a good one, they'll like that. Yes, Lily, you must do that one. We must publish it without delay. Have you got it written down, boy?"

Billy shook his head. "He ... he can't write music down," Lily said, trying to save Billy the embarrassment of admitting that he couldn't write words, either.

"Joe can write music. Joe, take it down, will you? Billy, go to Joe and sing it slowly, one line at a time. And Lily ... congratulations on finding this young man. He really is very talented."

Lily wanted to request that Billy should be given his own solo spot immediately, to sing the song, which was really a man's song, himself. But she knew better. She had just won one battle for Billy. The next one would have to wait, first, until they knew whether or not audiences liked his song, and second, until he showed a bit of gratitude! Didn't he realize what she had just done for him? He hadn't even said thank you! He was completely ungrateful. Lily felt very hurt.

She looked at him, standing next to Joe, his clothes grubby and unironed, his hair all over the place, his face animated as he played a melody line, then spoke the words slowly, while Joe matched them to the musical notes he had just written. He was totally exasperating, yet she felt a pang. He was so familiar to her, yet, in a way, so unknowable. What was going on in his heart of hearts? How did he spend his days? Why wouldn't he share things with her like he used to? Suggest that they met, went for walks? She would like to take him to lunch. She could afford to. But she knew that, in his present sulky mood, Billy would throw the invitation back in her face.

Nevertheless, she tried. When Joe announced that he now knew the song perfectly and had every word and note down on paper and would take it straight round to the publisher's, Billy promptly strapped his accordion on to his back.

"Billy, don't go yet!" Lily cried. "Don't you have to sign a contract if you're getting a song published? Anyway, I'm hungry. Come for some food with me!"

Billy gave her a look of haughty disdain. "I won't take crumbs from your table," he said, with bitterness in his voice.

"Be like that, then!" Lily shrugged, pain and anger burning inside her. How dare he insult her like that when she was truly only trying to be friends like they used to be?

Yet still she felt obliged to try one final time. "What's wrong, Billy? Why don't you want to know me any more?" she implored him, her voice breaking as she spoke. She missed him so much. He had been such a big part of her life. They had shared so much fun, so much music, all their hopes and dreams...

"We no longer inhabit the same world," he replied, meeting Lily's eyes steadily in a look which brought heat flooding to her face and set her body trembling.

Her voice was quavering as she responded, "If you are insinuating that I've gone up in the world through singing here, then all I can say is that pretty soon you'll be joining me on my lofty perch. Just as soon as your song is the hit that I feel sure it will be."

But Billy just repeated, "Different worlds, Lily," and left the theatre.

The moment he was gone, Lily stamped her foot. "Infuriating boy!" she shouted.

Joe gave her a sidelong glance from his seat at the piano, and adjusted the cravat he was wearing. "Damned handsome one, though, isn't he?" he said, staring to catch Lily's reaction.

Lily gave a haughty toss of her head. "Handsome is as handsome does. He's rude and ill-mannered," she said crossly.

When she saw Ned that evening, she kissed him in her dressing-room for longer, and with more passion, than usual, making up for Billy's hurtful behaviour.

Ned took this as encouragement to go further than he'd ever done before and wriggle his fingers inside her dress, reaching for her breasts.

"Don't! Stop it! Somebody might come in!" she protested. She tried to pull his hands away but he was stronger than she was and all she succeeded in doing was tearing a button off the bodice of her dress.

Ned appeared to find the ripping sound exciting and began to haul at her clothes as if attempting to wrench them all off her.

"No!" Lily screamed. Her door promptly burst open, as if on cue, and a lad popped his head in to say that Mr

Graydon would like a word with her before she went home, if she would be so kind.

She was embarrassed to be seen in such a dishevelled state, with her hair tumbling down and her clothing in disarray. No doubt the story, in exaggerated form, would be passed all round the other performers and backstage personnel.

Glaring at Ned, who appeared to have sunk into a sulk, she flung an embroidered silk shawl over her shoulders to cover the place where the button was missing, and went in search of her employer. *Men!* she fumed as she went. They would never do what you wanted them to. What was wrong with them? Her sisters might know. She would go and visit Edie and Millie very soon, and see if, by virtue of being married, they could shed any light on confusing male behaviour!

Chapter 14

Before consulting either Edie or Millie, Lily wrote to Elizabeth. She hadn't seen her since Mother's crisis, when the pale, terrified Elizabeth had arrived at the house after a long, complicated journey by cab and by train, sure that she would find her adored mother dead.

The reunion between Lily and her closest sister had been sweet and hearty. Once she had realized that their mother was out of danger, Elizabeth had relaxed and told Lily all the latest gossip about her governess job and her two troublesome charges. When Lily had broached the subject of sweethearts, Elizabeth had gone dreamy-eyed and said that there was a gentleman she was sweet on, but she had as yet received no signs that he returned her feelings.

"How can you tell if a man is interested in you?" she had asked Lily. Although completely inexperienced herself, Lily had informed Elizabeth about all the symptoms of love she had read in her romance books. But, in the weeks which had elapsed since Elizabeth had returned to Shropshire, she hadn't received one letter from her favourite sister.

Now she wrote:

26th April, 1899
Dearest Elizabeth,
    Guess what? I have a beau! His name is Ned Gates and he is a Sergeant in the Cavalry. He has brown hair which is very shiny and a splendid moustache. What progress have you made in your romance, Elizabeth? Please tell me, as I have realized that I do not understand men, not even Harry and Father, and the more I find out, the better.
    I am singing every night at the Old Mo and everyone is coming to see me on my birthday. Please, please ask your employer if he could spare you for a few days. It won't be the same if you're not there, and besides, you'll be able to meet Ned!
    Your loving sister, Lily.

She didn't expect an immediate reply, so she was pleasantly surprised when, just five days later, an envelope arrived addressed to her, with Elizabeth's writing on it.

My dearest Lily,
    I am so pleased that you have found love. So have I! I never thought I could be so happy. I blush to tell you the same of my sweetheart – nay, my fiancé! It is Mr Ingsby, my employer! Mrs Ingsby turned out not to be his wife, but his brother's widow, who, made homeless by her husband's death, came to lodge with my employer, whom I am still trying to get used to calling by his Christian name of Richard. I found out shortly after my arrival here, but never told Mother or Father for fear they should think I was in moral danger and demand my instant return.
    We are to be married in August and I shall tell Mother and

Father that not only are they gaining a son, but two "grand-children", my two little angels, Clarissa and Sam. Yes, I am like a mother to them now and they have fully accepted me. We all have so much fun.

I hope you will all come to our wedding, which will be here in St Peter's church on July 18th. I have asked Richard about your birthday concert party and we both hope to make the journey.

Your soon-to-be-wedded sister, Elizabeth. (Elizabeth Ingsby has a nice ring to it, don't you think?)

Lily Gates had a nice ring to it, too, thought Lily. Fancy Elizabeth marrying her employer! She was amused that the two little monsters had turned into angels now that Elizabeth was in love with their father. Mother would be so delighted. How was she to keep her mouth closed until Elizabeth's official letter arrived?

As it turned out, Lily had plenty of diversions. *Ship of Love* was a triumph. The first night she sang it, the applause went on for ages and she had to sing it twice more. The sheet music had been published and was selling fast. Billy should be receiving some money soon and perhaps that would make a difference to his mood and bring her those well overdue thanks, thought Lily.

One night, when Ned was in his usual box watching her performance, Lily gave an impromptu encore of *The Boy I Love Is Up In The Gallery*, directing the waves and kisses which customarily accompanied the song to "the gods", the cheapest seats at the very back of the theatre.

After the show, Ned came to collect her with a face like thunder. "You made a real fool of me, Lily, in front of my friends, too. They were all pulling my leg about it. How could you sing about the 'boy you love' and not wave at *me*? Everyone knows that we're going together!" he accused furiously.

Lily's hand flew to her mouth. "I didn't think!" she said. "It was just a song."

"Well, think of the words next time," he barked, and swept out to join his friends.

Immediately he had gone, the door of Lily's cupboard of a dressing-room burst open again. Standing there, still in her stage finery, was Sweet Jennie Brown, the current top of the bill star. Only the mood she was in now was far from sweet. In fact, the finger she waved at Lily was shaking with anger.

"How *dare* you?" she raged. "Who *do* you think you are? Everyone knows that *The Boy I Love* is *my* encore number! My audience expects it. And you had the utter cheek to steal it! You little ... upstart!"

Rushing up to Lily, she dealt her a stinging slap on the left cheek.

"I ... I'm sorry," Lily said faintly, still reeling from the attack. "It was the first song that popped into my head. I – I just didn't think."

It was the second time in five minutes that she had said those words, and each time they were connected to the same song.

Suddenly, her temper snapped and she jumped to her feet. "I hate that song!" She virtually spat the words into Sweet Jennie's liberally powdered face. "I hate it, I hate it! It's got me into trouble twice in one night and I'll never, *ever* sing it again."

"Good!" said Jennie brusquely, taking a step back from the wild-eyed fury who was confronting her. "That wasn't your soldier lad whom I just saw making great speed away from here, was it?" she asked tauntingly.

In her view, Lavender Blue was far too big for her boots and goodness only knew what an experienced manager like James Graydon saw in the plain little scrap. She could hold a tune all right, but she had no stage presence whatsoever and her inexperience showed. She would never last. She, Sweet Jennie Brown, would still be topping bills when Lavender Blue was sitting in a slum somewhere nursing a black eye and a crying baby! Such was the fate Sweet Jealous Jennie wished on her.

"So what if it was? It was just a little lovers' tiff." Lily spoke coolly. She was determined not to show her feelings to this horrible woman. Call herself a star? She was nothing but a collection of high-kicks and simpers. Maybe it was the colour of her garters that had won her so many admirers. It certainly couldn't have been her voice, which was as cracked as a vase dropped from a fourth-floor window, or her face, the heavy make-up on which accentuated rather than disguised her years, which had to be at least thirty-six.

Sweet Jennie Brown shrugged her be-ribboned shoulders. "Better mend that tiff quick, girl. Marguerite's been making eyes at him and everybody's sure he's been making them back," she informed Lily acidly. Marguerite was a pretty, blonde, French dancer whose high-kicks were even higher than Sweet Jennie's own, for which she was famous.

It was Lily's turn to shrug. "Then let him. I don't care. Plenty more fish in the sea," she said. She sat down again, turned round and ignored Jennie, who soon went. The moment she'd gone, Lily pounded her fist on her make-up table and shrieked, "Pig! Utter, detestable pig!", a statement which took in Jennie, Marguerite *and* Ned.

Next day, Ned made up for their first ever argument by presenting Lily with a most exquisite marcasite necklace in the shape of a lily of the valley.

"I'm sorry," he said, bowing low to kiss her hand. "I can't help feeling jealous when I see other men looking at you, or think you are looking at them. It's because I'm scared of losing you, Lily. There you are, up on stage every night with all those men gazing at you and wanting you. You could have your pick of any of them!"

"But I don't want them, Ned, I want you," Lily said gently.

Ned leapt up and swept her into his arms, raining kisses all over her hair and face. "Oh Lily, I do love you so very much," he muttered into her hair. "Do you love me?"

"Of course I do!" replied an astonished Lily, an agreeable glow spreading through her. *He loves me ... he's just said it! Oh, how I wish Elizabeth were here!* she thought. Elizabeth's letter to her parents had arrived and they were delighted by her news. How would they feel if there were to be *two* weddings in the family?

"I keep forgetting how young you are," Ned said, stopping his caresses. "But you will be seventeen soon. And then, in another year, you will be eighteen and I could think about... Well, I could think about..."

"Think about what?" urged Lily, a mist forming in front of her eyes. She knew what he was about to say. It was to be a proposal, just as she had been dreaming about!

"Nothing, my dear." Ned cleared his throat.

"Are you sure?" asked Lily urgently, placing a hand on his arm.

He clutched her hand and held on to it. "Lily," he said, "the purpose of being a soldier is to do one's duty for one's country. From time to time, rumours of trouble come from various parts of the world. There is one such trouble spot brewing at the moment. I can't mention where it is as all despatches are top secret, but it is a long way from England. We all hope that it will be settled soon, but if it isn't, my regiment will have to go there and I could be away for a long time. Even if you were all of twenty, it would be unfair and unreasonable for me to ask you to become engaged under those circumstances. But at your age ... I wouldn't do it, my dear. Do you understand?"

Go away? With his regiment? He might get killed! White with horror, Lily stared at Ned. His familiar features dissolved into those of a pallid corpse. His eyes became empty pits from which clots of blood had run and dried in dark blobs. His lovely, warm mouth was a frozen gash, twisted in the agony of death.

"Lily, what's the matter?"

She shook her head, dispelling the foul vision. "Nothing. Just a nasty feeling. Someone must have walked over my grave." She was referring to the belief that when someone walked over the grave of the person you were in a previous existence, the person you were in this life got the cold shivers.

Ned put his arm round her and gave her a cuddle. "Come on, don't be sad. Nothing's going to happen to your Ned, he's too big and brave and strong. I'm a jolly good soldier, you know, and a superb horseman. You ask any of my friends and family. Nothing unseats me. I'll get the better of any opponent on the field. Don't like being too close to the cannons, though. Hurts my delicate ears!"

He grimaced and rubbed his ears and Lily gave the laugh that was expected of her. But there was no amusement in her heart.

Lily's seventeenth birthday came round at last. Her mother, wearing the spectacles which Lily had bought her, which had restored perfect sight and banished her headaches, had baked a cake and iced it in lavender-coloured icing. Millie and Edie had been cooking, too, and had called at the house that afternoon with pastries and savoury dishes. And, best of all, Elizabeth had come, shyly clutching the hand of Richard, who turned out to be a quiet, bearded, kindly chap of around forty years old, to whom everyone took an instant liking.

Later, George and Gerald arrived. Lily had asked to be spared her first house performance that night, and her spot had been given to a newcomer, a young comedian, allowing her to spend more time with her family.

As the hour drew near for her big performance, she grew more and more nervous. She had expanded her act to six songs, two of which were Billy's – she was singing his song about the Welsh girl, too.

They were all to be seated in Ned's box. Lily set out for the theatre first, to allow herself time to get ready. As she neared the entrance, a grey bowler hat and lilac waistcoat caught her eye.

"Jago!" she cried delightedly, throwing her arms around him and hugging him.

139

Flushed and beaming, the stout man wished her a very happy birthday and gave her a small package, instructing her not to open it until later.

"I'll go now, m'dear," he said in his bluff way. "I won't intrude on your family gathering."

"But you mustn't go!" Lily protested. "You must stay and hear me sing, you promised! Come…"

She took him up to the box and opened the door. "The others will be along in twenty minutes or so. I've told them about you. They're expecting to meet you," she said as an added inducement.

Whether it was the knowledge that everybody she loved most was in the audience, or because it was her birthday, Lily sang her heart out that night and was called up to deliver not one, but a dozen encores. It was a full twenty minutes before she was allowed to leave the stage, so enthusiastic were the cheers and the applause.

Her family and friends waited in the foyer for her to emerge and were lavish with their praise and congratulations. Ned took her hand and Lily felt proud to walk along with him, noting that Elizabeth was holding Richard's hand. She felt as if she and Ned were officially engaged already.

It wasn't until the party had broken up and Elizabeth and Richard had left to spend the night with Edie and George, that Lily remembered the small package she had been given by Jago. She yawned wearily as her fingernails scrabbled at the knot in the scarlet string that had been used to tie it. She couldn't untie it and was forced to cut it with the vegetable knife.

Taking off the paper, she opened the small box that it had adorned and there, gleaming on a pad of blue tissue paper, was one of Jago's special medallions bearing the portrait of himself on one side and the harp on the other. Beneath the harp was inscribed her name, Lily, and rather than being silver like the others, this medallion was made of the purest gold.

Dear Jago, Lily thought, pressing the cold, precious metal to her cheek. Despite the sapphire brooch she had received from Ned, the pretty clothes from her sisters, the new, hand-made summer coat from her mother, the books from her father and the pretty mother-of-pearl mirror from Harry, Jago's present was the best of all.

Chapter 15

The thought that Ned might soon be called away was always in Lily's mind, not constantly at the forefront of her thoughts, but simmering away in the background. Maybe it was the fear that she might be parted from him soon that caused Lily's feelings for him to grow daily more intense.

"Oh Lily, Lily," he murmured into her hair one evening as he walked her home from the theatre, "I really am most serious about you, you know."

"I should hope you are!" she said, giving him a flick with one of the fine leather gloves she held in her hand. Although it was late June, the weather that windy evening was far from warm.

"I think a visit to my parents is long overdue," he informed her. "I have told them about you, but it isn't easy to convince them that a music-hall singer can be a nice, well brought up girl who would make a suitable wife for a man of my standing."

"Oh!" Colour flamed and faded in Lily's insulted cheeks. How could they think such a thing?

She checked her angry thoughts as the sad realization dawned that Ned's parents' opinion was the one held by almost everybody. Everyone assumed that girls who were on the stage were daily exposed to licentiousness, courted by scores of men, tempted by rich gifts to surrender their honour, and couldn't possibly be "nice girls".

"When do you want this ordeal to take place?" she enquired, a trifle acidly.

"What ordeal?" asked Ned in surprise.

"The ordeal of having to prove myself a fit lady friend for the son of shipping and wine magnate Lionel Gates," Lily said, staring him haughtily in the eyes. Her dander was up now, and Ned had better be careful what he said or they might just have their second lovers' tiff!

Ned didn't rise to the bait. Instead, he burst out laughing and rubbed his moustache vigorously as he composed a reply.

"My parents aren't ogres," he informed her. "They're just ordinary, decent folk, a bit wealthier than some, who are anxious to protect their fortune and their standards."

"And they think that someone like me would spend all their fortune and bring their good name into disrepute, I suppose." Lily was still angry – and even angrier when he reached out and ruffled her hair like someone caressing a pet dog.

Ned laughed even more heartily. "Oh, Lily, I do wish you had a glass and could see yourself," he spluttered. "Your face! The look in your eyes! You look like a proud peacock whose tail has just been stepped on."

"Me? A peacock? I'm not remotely like a peacock!" Lily shouted. Her temper was on the point of exploding altogether and she had to work hard to prevent herself stamping her foot like a petulant child, or drumming on his chest with her fists.

"You are when you're all puffed up like this!" he said, his eyes glinting with tears of suppressed mirth.

"You ... you *beast*!" Unable to restrain herself any longer, she took a swing at him. Ned caught her wrist in a twisting grip which was far too strong and hurt her so much that she yelped in pain.

With a startled, apologetic look, he let her go and she rubbed her wrist and arm, staring at him with large, injured eyes.

"I'm sorry. I don't know my own strength sometimes," he said gruffly. "Are you all right?"

"It's just as well that I only sing and don't have to play an instrument, otherwise I would be looking for an accompanist tomorrow," she replied stiffly.

Ned put his arm round her shoulders. "From now on, I shall treat you as if you were made of glass. Fragile Venetian glass. It's very beautiful but breaks at the slightest knock," he said.

"I don't break as easily as that," Lily assured him.

Ned cleared his throat. "I thought that perhaps on Sunday week... We have a beautiful garden leading down to the river. If the weather is pleasant, we could take the boat out."

"That would be lovely," Lily found herself saying, against her will. "What should I wear?"

"Something plain and suitable for the country. Green, perhaps. My mother believes that country clothes should blend in with Nature. She always wears browns and greens and the occasional blue, but never pink or red. She saves that for town."

"But poppies are red and roses are pink! Geraniums are

red, too!" Lily protested, thinking what a peculiar woman Ned's mother must be. She was thoroughly dreading the forthcoming visit...

Her mood was made even worse by a chance encounter with Billy Morgan. Lily had taken Archie out for some air, to give her mother some peace and quiet, and they were just returning home along New Oxford Street when she saw Billy coming out of a music publisher's in Denmark Street.

Fearing an unpleasant confrontation, she looked away and pretended that she hadn't seen him and that she was occupied with the heavy baby she was carrying. But it was too late. Billy crossed the street and stood in front of her, stopping her in her tracks.

"Hello, stranger. Too high and mighty to talk to me now?" he challenged.

Lily's temper flared. " 'Hello stranger', yourself!" she fired back at him. "Don't try and blame me. You've been the one who has been avoiding me, not the other way round. Where have you been?"

"Oh, here and there," he said annoyingly.

Lily's heart gave a jump. She was suddenly acutely aware of his height, of his good looks, his pale, bony features which were so different from Ned's ruddy, hearty complexion. He was standing with his back to the sun and his untidy black curls shone in the sunlight, but his eyes were lost in shadow, dark and enigmatic, his expression impossible to read. Was he extending the hand of friendship at last, or was he merely mocking her?

She soon found out. "I failed to recognize your little brother. For a moment, I thought you had become a mother yourself," he said, with a perfectly straight face.

Lily had never been so insulted in her life. If she had had a free hand, she would have slapped him, but both her arms were occupied in restraining Archie, who was wriggling and complaining as he wanted to be put down where he could crawl, but the pavements were far too filthy to allow it.

Billy stood there, watching her speechless fury. Try as she might, she couldn't think of anything bad enough to say to him.

"What's wrong? Can't you take a joke any more? I would have thought that mixing with soldiers would have broadened your sense of humour," he taunted, with an emphasis on the word "broadened".

Lily decided to play him along. Arching an eyebrow, she said, "One thing it's taught me is never to waste your fire-power on an enemy not worth fighting."

Billy's mouth dropped open, then a grin spread across his face. "Touché!" he exclaimed. "Well done, Lily." He started laughing and suddenly, with a great sense of release from tension, laughter bubbled up inside Lily, too. In fact, she laughed so hard that she almost dropped Archie, who waved protesting arms and legs until Billy took him from her and raised him to the sky with a shout, then swung him down almost to pavement level, making him gurgle and squeal.

His arms looked strong and muscular as he played games with the child. All at once, Lily became acutely aware of his body. It was as if a power emanated from him that spoke directly to her own body. Confusion spread through her as she dimly recalled other times when she had felt this way towards Billy. Walking down Brook Street after visiting Mrs Booth-Edwards… On the boat…

What's wrong with me? she wondered. *I'm walking out with Ned, so how can I feel this way about Billy? Billy doesn't even like me any more, he's made that quite clear. He doesn't see that I've grown up, he thinks I'm still a funny little girl who he can tease and taunt. If I had pigtails, he'd be pulling them.*

"What were you doing in the music publishing house?" she asked him, desperate to dispel her disturbing feelings.

Billy placed Archie on his shoulders and held him there while the baby crowed with delight. "I've found someone who can write out my songs for me, the words and the music. Each time I make up a new one, I get it written down so that I can take it around the theatres and find someone to sing it," he explained.

Lily felt shocked. So she wasn't the only one singing Billy Morgan's songs, which she had always felt were exclusive to her, on account of their old friendship.

"I see," she said. "I hope no one is singing the songs you have given to me."

Billy looked at her in surprise. "Songs are for everybody, Lily. They're universal," he said. "If everyone in the world sang songs of mine, I'd be really happy."

"I thought that when you gave me a song, like *Ship of Love*, for instance, you gave it to me and to nobody else," she said.

"I gave it to you first. If someone hears you sing it and wants to sing it themselves, that's up to them," he said. "How many different singers do, *How Much Is That Doggy In The Window?*"

"I don't know. Lots, I suppose."

"There you are, then," he said cheerfully. "Songs get passed on like that and if you're lucky, they live for ever. Look at *Lavender Blue*."

"You just want to make money," she accused him.

"And why not? You're making money, aren't you? Surely you wouldn't begrudge the songwriter a few shillings, too?" he said with a laugh.

This time Lily couldn't join in the laughter. Something had been lost – something very special. Something that had existed just between Billy and herself. Trouble was, she wasn't sure what it even was! She couldn't put up with this encounter any longer. It had grown uncomfortable, as encounters with Billy always did, sooner or later.

"I must go," she said. "Give me Archie, please."

"There you go, Archie *bach*. Go to your big sister," he crooned to the baby. As he handed him over, Billy's hand brushed hers and she felt her flesh burn where they touched. It made her feel angry. How dare he have this effect on her, when he said such horrible things to her?

"Thanks," she muttered. "Goodbye. And I want you to think of me first next time you write a new song."

Billy cheekily touched an invisible cap. "Yes, Miss Lavender," he said and walked off, leaving Lily wondering if she had indeed spoken to him in the imperious tones of a music-hall star. Or was he trying to get a rise out of her again, and get in the last word? With Billy, you just never knew.

The Sunday of Lily's visit to Ned's parents dawned blazingly hot. Lily took the train from Waterloo and arrived at Kingston-Upon-Thames feeling dusty and creased.

Ned had said he would meet her but she certainly didn't expect the newly painted gig with the brass lamps gleaming and the white horse with blue ribbons plaited into his mane and tail. Ned was sitting there, whip in hand, a white silk scarf tied dashingly around his sun-burned neck.

Hampered by the long green velvet skirt of her costume, and choked by her high-necked ruffled blouse, Lily made heavy weather of scrambling into the vehicle. But once they were bumping down the road at what seemed like an incredible speed, Lily, cooled by the breeze, started to enjoy the ride.

"Is this yours?" she asked Ned.

"No, it's my father's. It's the coachman's day off. I shall have my own personal carriage and horses when I leave the Cavalry."

"What do you mean, 'leave the Cavalry'?" Lily enquired. "I thought you intended to become Colonel of a regiment in India?"

Ned's mouth drew into a thin line. "It's Father," he said abruptly. "The doctors have told him he mustn't work so hard. His heart. He had a bad turn recently. So I have decided to resign my commission once these troubles are over and take over the business, which is what Father has always wanted."

"How about your brother?"

"Phillip has no head for business. He's a playboy. He's never at home. Always running around with women. I hear he is in Paris right now, indulging himself at the Folies Bergère. I shall cut off his allowance and make him work for a change, you see if I don't!"

"It sounds as if you'll have to catch him first," Lily remarked.

Ned's only answer was a grunt as he pulled the reins sharply to the right and turned into a sweeping drive lined with horse chestnut trees whose branches were heavy with white, blossomy candles.

Lily's mouth formed a silent "O" of admiration as she saw the house which they were approaching. The proportions of its white, Georgian façade were unmarred by any ugly side additions. Gleaming pillars flanked the doorway. Ned jumped down and offered a helping hand to Lily. The door opened and a maid stood there. As Lily and Ned approached, she bobbed her head demurely.

"The Master and Madam are in the garden. Lunch will be served on the lawn in half an hour," she informed them.

Lily tried hard to hide her awe as she passed across the lofty, spacious hall. Fancy having so much room for just one family! The walls were hung with ancient and no doubt valuable oil paintings in heavy gilt frames. A wide marble staircase with ornately carved banisters swept majestically upwards from the centre of the hallway and split into two sections, one curving left and one right. Bright sunlight shining through the landing window created a blinding, slightly misty effect, as if Lily were seeing it in a dream.

She blinked and glanced once again at the maid, who was ushering her towards a door on the left. She followed Ned into a wide drawing-room with a golden Chinese carpet. French windows led to a conservatory in which a large vine twisted and tumbled across the roof. Through the glass, Lily glimpsed a table and sunshades. Two people were involved in a game of croquet. Others were sitting talking, or admiring the verdant plants which fringed a large pond over which a pale, silvery willow drooped its feathery fronds.

"Damn! That's the Allisons. Why did Mother have to invite them?" grumbled Ned.

"Who are the Allisons?" Lily enquired.

"You'll find out soon enough. Mad woman, completely barmy. Spiritualist or something. Insufferable husband. A complete bore. I don't know what Mother sees in them."

"Er … which ones are your parents?" asked Lily nervously.

Ned pointed to a seated couple. The woman had silver hair piled on top of her head in a series of curls the size of cream puffs. She was quite stout and was, as Ned predicted, wearing green, though a far paler shade than Lily's, which was more of an olive colour. Ned's father looked thin and frail. Despite the heat, he had a plaid woollen blanket draped over his shoulders.

Suddenly, an exquisite golden-haired girl, dressed all in white, came running towards them, her long skirts hitched up in one hand, showing her slender, white-stockinged legs.

"Ned, Ned, you've brought her!" She gazed at Lily with shining eyes.

"Lily, meet my little sister, Susannah," Ned said. "Susannah, this is Miss Lily Cobbett."

"You're the famous Lavender Blue! You look just like your portrait in *London Life*," gasped the girl admiringly.

Lily didn't even know that her portrait had appeared in any magazine, but she remained tactfully silent on that point, smiled warmly at the young girl, who must have been around fourteen, and allowed herself to be kissed on the cheek.

Susannah commandeered her, plying her with questions about what being on stage in front of an audience felt like and whether she had ever met the wicked Marie Lloyd. Lily answered as best she could under the circumstances, which were that Susannah was steering her gradually over to the table where her parents sat. Mr Gates went to stand but his wife pushed him firmly back into his chair. She pursed her lips as her gimlet eyes stabbed over every aspect of Lily's face, hair, body and clothing. She never found out whether or not her outfit had passed muster. All she got was a slight nod and a wave of the hand directing her to a place at the far end of the table.

Lily had never felt more nervous in her life. This was worse than her audition with James Graydon. She felt sure that, before the day was out, she was bound to blot her copybook in one way or another, and never be admitted to the Gates' household again.

"Oh, Mother," Lily said later as she sat dreamily in the kitchen, "it was a lovely day. Ned's parents were rather cold, but the wonderful trip on the river made up for it!"

Although she had been brought up close to the Thames, Lily had never actually sailed. The only boat she had ever been on was Billy's, which hadn't gone anywhere. Ned's rowing boat had floated her up the glittering water, past banks of lush grass, past swans, herons and moorhens, while she sat lazily on the bench at the back, trailing one hand in the water, until Ned announced that he was tired and it was her turn to take the oars.

"What do I do?" she asked in alarm.

"Stand up and walk very carefully to where I am sitting.

I'll change seats with you. Keep the oars in the rowlocks, scoop them backwards shallowly and pull. Don't dig them into the water or you're likely to catch a crab and overturn the boat."

"I've never seen a crab big enough to overturn a rowing boat," Lily said innocently, and wondered why Ned started laughing.

Once she had got into the rhythm of it, she found she really enjoyed rowing. Steering a straight line was difficult, though, especially when you were going backwards and the river kept bending.

"Why can't they put a mirror in the boat so that you can see where you are heading?" she complained.

"Boats never have mirrors. You just have to look where you're going, or let me guide you. Left! Pull hard on your right oar, there's an overhanging branch coming up."

Having registered his call of "Left", Lily made the mistake of tugging on her left oar. The next moment, something tangled in her hair and pulled her off her seat.

"Ouch!" she screamed, as her hair was severely pulled and the fragile craft rocked alarmingly.

"Keep calm, don't panic. You hair's caught on some twigs," Ned said. Crawling over to Lily, he gently disentangled her – and then, while his fingers were still enmeshed in her long, soft hair, he moved his lips towards hers for a kiss.

A pool of water lay in the bottom of the boat but Lily didn't notice her skirts getting wet as she sank down in Ned's embrace. His hands daringly roamed over her breasts. Her breathing became ragged as his touch kindled wicked, forbidden flickers within her body.

"Don't ... *please!*" she begged, trying to prise his hands away from her bosom.

"Why not, my darling? We're to be married, after all," Ned said hoarsely. She felt the hard length of his body pressing and moving against hers.

"*Don't,*" she implored again. Then the trancelike state into which she had sunk evaporated like mist on the water and she abruptly sat up, causing the boat to rock violently. "Married? But you haven't even asked me properly yet," she complained.

Ned knelt in the puddle at the bottom of the boat. "Lily Cobbett, please will you marry me?" he said and, as if from a great distance, she faintly heard herself whisper, "Yes..."

"He got wet knees and I had a damp seat!" Lily giggled. "I think our clothes blotted up all the water in the boat. But we'd dried out by the time we got back."

"How did his parents take the news?" Cecily Cobbett wanted to know.

Lily bit her lip and her eyes met her mother's as she gave a small, rueful grimace of apology on his behalf. "He ... he hasn't told them yet," she said.

"Why ever not?" her mother demanded.

"He says that as they've only just made my acquaintance, we should wait a bit until they know me better and can see what a suitable wife I will make," she said, in a tone which didn't sound completely convinced.

Cecily certainly wasn't. Indeed, she was indignant on her youngest daughter's behalf. "What a puffed-up lot of self-important emptyheads they sound!" she said. "I think

154

I'd rather not have them as relatives by marriage, if that's what they're really like."

"I'm sure they'll be perfectly nice once we've all got used to one another," Lily said sensibly. "It must have been a shock to them to hear that their son and heir was in love with a showgirl."

"You're not a showgirl!" protested her mother. "You're a singer with an exquisite voice – an artiste! You're far better than them, my girl, and maybe you could do far better than Ned. You don't have to marry a man just because he asks you, you know. After all, he's only the first. There may be many more – dukes, earls and princes amongst them!"

She stopped, realizing she might have gone too far. But, far from rounding on her, Lily's face was dreamy, her mind enwrapped in a happy trance, her unfocused eyes seeing only the rosy images conjured up by love – she and Ned cruising down sunny lanes in a shiny motor car, or rowing down a silvery river, sitting side by side with an oar each.

"I don't want princes and earls," she said softly. "Ned Gates will do just fine."

Chapter 16

The next evening, Ned wasn't in the audience for the second house. She knew that he had many responsibilities, both to his regiment and to his father, and even to his friends, and that he couldn't be at the Old Mo every single time she appeared. But there was something about his absence on the very day after he had proposed to her, which filled her with foreboding.

As she changed out of her stage dress and took off her make-up, she found her ears were straining for the sound of his familiar knock on her dressing-room door. Rat-*TAT* … tat, with a pause between the second and loudest knock and the quieter third one. But this night it didn't come and Lily left the theatre alone.

Perhaps he had told his parents of their engagement and they had objected and made him vow never to see her again, she thought anxiously. The news, when it came, was even worse than that. Lily was just washing her face and getting ready for bed at eleven o'clock when Harry announced that they had a late-night visitor. It was Ned. Grim-faced, he waved a handful of papers at her.

"My orders," he said gruffly. "My regiment is going on military training. You may have read in the newspapers about trouble brewing in South Africa. The Boers are threatening to rise against British rule. I have to leave tomorrow. We may be sailing soon."

Lily felt her face grow white. It was as if all the strength in her body was draining out through the soles of her feet. She managed a weak, "Oh," and sank down into a chair while her mother put an arm round her shoulders.

"So I won't see you again?" she said. Then, realizing that she sounded as if she were signing his death warrant, she added, "Until you're home on leave, I mean."

Ned nodded grimly. "I'm afraid not. But never fear, I'm sure it won't lead to anything. The government is just taking precautions. And I'll write to you, you can be sure of that."

Murmuring something about making some tea, Lily's mother tactfully retreated to the kitchen, taking Harry and Charlie with her.

The minute they were alone, Ned took Lily's hands and sank to his knees before her.

"As soon as I return, I will give you an engagement ring," he said. "My maternal grandmother left a beautiful ruby, with instructions that it was to be worn by my mother's first son's wife. However, I have been unable to persuade Mother to part with it yet. It is her favourite jewel."

Lily wasn't over-fond of rubies. She thought they resembled drops of blood. Sapphires were her favourite jewels. So, secretly, she was quite pleased with Mrs Gates' reluctance to part with her heirloom.

"Promise you'll write to me?" Ned begged. "Please, my darling Lily? Your letters will enable me to survive the horrors of the battlefield. If I come back in one piece, with body and soul intact, it will be down to you."

It was an awesome responsibility, but Lily promised.

Ned got to his feet. He gathered Lily to him and gave her such a kiss that she felt he would draw out her soul through her lips. "I must go now. Farewell, sweetheart, until we meet again. I'll think of you every second."

On the doorstep, they clung to each other so tightly that not even the thinnest sword blade could have squeezed between them. Then Ned pushed Lily gently away.

"Take care while I am gone, Lily – my Lavender Blue. If I find any lavender on the battlefields, I shall bring a sprig back for you. Although I hope I shall return safely without seeing a battlefield."

"I'll sing a song for you every night..." whispered Lily.

"And I shall hear it, never fear, even above the thunder of the cannons."

Lily gave a shudder as he said this. Cannons ... horses screaming and falling ... soldiers bleeding and dying in agony. She shook her head to clear the terrible image and formed a positive one in its place, of Ned returning hale, whole and hearty and the two of them proceeding into church beneath an arch of linked peacetime sword blades, to be married at last.

It was strange not seeing Ned in his familiar box, with his group of uproarious friends. In her subdued state, Harry became her escort, turning up loyally after every perform-ance to see off troublesome "stage-door Johnnies" and to walk her safely home.

As August drew on, Lily found consolation in someone whom, the previous summer, she would never have thought it possible to communicate with – Archie, her baby brother.

Archie had grown into a very fine, bonny toddler indeed. He had a thick head of hair now, which was a beautiful burnished auburn in shade – "Just like mine was when I was a boy," his father declared proudly.

Indeed, Mr Cobbett often captured his small son and whisked him away to show him off to his friends from the market.

"Archie is a good influence on him," said Cecily smugly, as Charlie Cobbett began spending less time in the inn and more time with his darling boy.

Archie was a good influence on everybody, thought Lily. The whining, semi-starved baby had become a happy, winsome infant whose sunny personality and chuckly laugh never failed to raise a smile in all who came into contact with him. Lily loved taking him for a walk each day. Sometimes their mother would accompany them but, more often than not, she would be working on a new collection of outfits for one of her growing army of clients, aided by the new spectacles and sewing machine provided by Lily.

Lily had by now deposited her cash in the bank, rather than continuing to bury it secretly beneath the floor-boards. Every time she studied her bankbook, she was thrilled to see how much her savings had grown. Soon, very soon, she would be able to put her dearest wish into action, and that was to move her family out of the two cramped top rooms in Mrs Molloy's house and into their very own home, with its own lavatory shared by no other household. What bliss that would be!

Harry had broken off with Dora and was now courting Ellen, a girl who worked in a shoe shop. She had given both him and his father a goodly discount off a pair of new brogues each, and Charlie pronounced her ideal as a dutiful daughter-in-law. Lily wasn't so sure, though. Compared to the cheeky, sparkly Dora, Ellen was a dull thing, with her long, pointed nose, straight brown hair and mud-coloured eyes. When she visited, she had scarcely anything to say for herself. She was like a mouse – no, a shrew, with that long nose and brown colouring. Lily half expected her to sprout whiskers and start squeaking any day.

Ellen must have had something to recommend her, though, because Harry soon pronounced himself engaged to her and informed the family that they would save up and marry in two years' time, when he would be twenty-one and Ellen, who was a year older than him, twenty-two.

"What do *you* think of her?" Lily asked her mother. She had always valued her mother's opinion, knowing that Cecily operated with a mixture of observation and intuition that was seldom wrong.

"Never judge a book by its cover," Cecily said cheerfully. "That girl has hidden depths. She reads a lot, you know. She's a thinker. And Harry says she's an excellent cook. She's no flibbertigibbet like that Dora was. I think she'll make him a good wife."

"But she's so *quiet*!" Lily protested.

"Just what your brother needs. Imagine if they were both equally talkative and noisy. Neither would ever get a word in edgeways. Ellen is a good foil for his personality. She's prepared to stay in the background and let him shine, like the dark cloth beneath a diamond. But she's a good organizer and good with figures. Mark my words, their household will never be in debt."

After this, Lily set out to be as friendly as possible towards Ellen and found that the girl gradually opened up to her and that they could even share some thoughts and some laughs. It was good to have a sister again. Lily hadn't realized how much she had missed Elizabeth, who had been her best friend and closest companion as well as her sister.

Harry took Ellen to the wedding of Elizabeth and Richard, which took place at the start of September, the wedding having been delayed in order to allow Richard's young son, Sam, time to get over an attack of mumps.

The weather was capricious, with bright sunshine one moment and showers the next. "I hope our life together will be like this," Elizabeth told Lily happily. "A mixture of everything. Not sun all the time, not rain all the time, but plenty of change and interest. Have you heard anything from Ned, by the way?"

"I had a note three days ago," Lily confided. "He says he is about to set sail and that they will be at sea for three and a half weeks, and that I shouldn't worry if I don't hear from him until they reach dry land."

She had kept the page, written in pencil on official paper, tucked inside her bag, but now that she and Elizabeth were sitting in the large marquee which had been erected on the Ingsby lawn, tucking into tiny, delicious strawberry tartlets which a curtseying Clarissa, Elizabeth's nine-year-old step-daughter, had offered them, she snapped open her grey kid leather bag and took out the carefully folded letter.

"He doesn't say very much, but at least he says he misses me," she remarked, handing it to her sister. She had been very disappointed by the letters she had received. They gave no information about where he was or what he was doing, and Lily wanted to know every little detail, so that she could live through his experiences with him.

Elizabeth read it in silence, then gave it back to Lily. "I shouldn't worry about him not saying much, they're not allowed to, you know. It's army rules. They're not allowed to say exactly where they are in case the enemy finds out."

"How do you know?" Lily enquired.

"Oh, Richard's first cousin is Colonel Horace Ingsby. Perhaps you've heard of him?"

"Of course!" Lily said. "Ned has spoken of him. Well, fancy you and he being cousins by marriage!" Lily paused, then ventured, "I don't suppose there is any way in which my correspondence with Ned could be speeded up, by sending it via the Colonel?" She was aware that she might be taking liberties in asking the question, but Elizabeth didn't seem to mind.

"I'll ask Richard and see if he thinks it's possible," she said.

Lily gave a deep sigh. Oh, lucky Elizabeth, to be having such a perfect wedding day. Would her own be anything like this? Indeed, would it take place at all? Heaven only knew whether or not a war was about to break out – and if it did, who could tell how long it might last?

As if reading her mind, Elizabeth said, "I feel so sorry for you, Lily dear. You must be so worried. At least I can keep Richard here at my side. There is no chance of him being pressed into the Army or the Navy, as he is far too old."

She smiled mischievously and Lily endeavoured to smile back, though she felt tears threatening her eyes. At last she was talking to somebody who truly understood. Elizabeth had always been like that – intuitive, sympathetic. Oh, how she missed her!

Her older sister patted her hand and gave her an encouraging smile. "Come now, we are neglecting the other guests," she said. "There's Edie over there. I must have a word with her. Come with me."

"In a moment," Lily promised, feeling she needed a few moments to regain her composure after her fit of melancholy.

After Elizabeth had gone to rejoin her husband and take up her new social position as the second Mrs Ingsby, a sombre Lily remained seated and brooding. Elizabeth's information about army regulations concerning the content of letters had gone part of the way to explaining the strange sense of detachment she had got from Ned's note. Despite his affirmation of love, she had found his words impersonal and had got no warm, secret thrill from them.

There and then, she attempted to reach out to him with her thoughts. She summoned up a sharp, clear picture of Ned's face, with his sparkling brown eyes, gleaming hair, high colour and the flourishing moustache which accentuated the sensual curves of his lips. *Dear Ned*, she projected silently, *I hope you are all right. I love you. Please God, don't let there be any fighting. Stay alive for me, Ned, please…*

Chapter 17

News of the territorial squabbles in South Africa between the British and the Boers had been in the papers for weeks and war was officially declared on October 10th, 1899. Every day, Lily waited to see if she would get a letter from Ned, but nothing came. At first, the war seemed to be going against the British and the papers carried reports of heavy defeats. Lily was worried sick. Casualty lists were printed and she could scarcely bear to look in case the name, *Gates, Sgt. N.,* leapt off the page at her.

As the weeks went on without any sign of his name, she began to relax. After all, no news meant good news, didn't it? Finally, towards the end of November, a letter came, just a short note, smudged and crumpled, which said: *Many casualties but I am all right, thanks be. We're moving on today, so no time for long letter. This will let you know I am still alive, at least. Your loving Ned.*

Lily clutched it to her, feeling as if she would explode with happiness and that evening she dedicated a song to "all our brave boys who are fighting to defend our territories in South Africa".

Next morning, as she was running through a new arrangement with Joe, he produced a sheet of manuscript paper and said, "Mr Graydon gave me this. He thinks it's rather appropriate, with the war an' all."

He handed Lily the songsheet. The song was called, *My Heart Is With You, Soldier Lad* and as she read the words, she felt they could have been written just for her and Ned.

"Who wrote this?" she asked Joe.

"Billy Morgan. He brought it in yesterday afternoon."

Billy! She might have known. "Play it for me, Joe," she said and as he played the melody, she read the words from the sheet of paper in her hand. The chorus went:

My heart is with you, soldier lad, as you march into battle.
I'm by your side as cannons roar and clashing sabres rattle.
You have my love to keep you safe as war around you
   screams.
And every night I hold you tight and kiss you in my dreams.

Damn you, Billy Morgan! she thought furiously. It was as if he were playing a cruel, sadistic game with her, torturing her emotions. News of her engagement to Ned couldn't have failed to reach his ears. Everyone at the Old Mo knew about it and so did Jago, as Lily had specially sought him out to tell him.

Jago's reaction hadn't been at all what Lily had expected. Rather than seeming happy for her, he had wrinkled his brow and given her a look which seemed dubious rather than delighted. All he had said was, "Well, Lily, I know that all young ladies want a husband and I'm sure that if you think Ned is the right one for you, then he must be. I wish you well, my dear," and had immediately returned to his newspaper.

Lily had left the coffee shop feeling greatly disappointed

and robbed of the congratulations she had felt were her due. *Silly old man*, she had thought crossly. What does he know about love? He has a wife, but still, the moment he first fell in love with her must be so long ago now that he is bound to have forgotten what it felt like. Or perhaps she had just caught him at a bad moment, when he had other things on his mind.

Cheered slightly by her conclusions, she had continued to her destination, which was to the draper's to buy some frogging for a military-style jacket which her mother was creating.

Later that day, she sat in her bedroom with the words of *My Heart Is With You, Soldier Lad*, singing it quietly over and over as she committed it to memory. Strangely, though, as she sang it wasn't Ned's face that danced before her eyes but Billy Morgan's – that cheeky grin, those bright, soulful eyes, that uncontrollable mop of curls and waves, those expressive features which mapped his swiftly changing moods, street urchin one minute, poet the next. Billy was unique. Compared to him, every other male of her acquaintance was totally—

A jolt of alarm shot through Lily and she abruptly stopped singing, shocked by the drift of her thoughts. The word that had been about to form in her mind was… No, she daren't think about it. She must squash it, erase it, before it did any damage to her memory of Ned. Yet, like a nasty, hard-to-kill bug, it wriggled its way back into her mind again. The word was "boring".

No, no! she berated herself. Ned wasn't at all boring. He was mature, confident. He wasn't a petulant, moody boy like Billy, he was a wonderful, strong, responsible man who knew his own mind. He was dashingly handsome, possessed of a fine figure. He had marvellous prospects. He was amusing, attentive, thoughtful and caring.

She thought of the way he held back his passion, broke off their kisses before he was tempted to go further in his lovemaking. He was controlled, whereas Billy ... Billy was like a wild mountain stream, uncheckable, tumbling where it would, over boulders, between banks, sometimes carving fresh courses for itself by flowing over obstacles in its path. Images of the uncontrollable forces of Nature often came to her when she thought about Billy. Thinking of Ned produced images of formal balls with the ladies in fashionable gowns and the men in uniform, of strolls in town with them both dressed in their best clothes.

Stop haunting me, Billy Morgan, Lily ordered him in her thoughts. *Let me go. You're in the past now. And as for your songs, forget what I said and let another girl sing them!*

But she knew she couldn't bear that to happen. *Soldier Lad* was the best new song she had heard in ages. Although it wreaked havoc with her peace of mind, she couldn't not sing it. Her fame and Billy's were interlinked, whether she liked it or not.

Christmas was drawing near and Lily found herself missing Ned more and more. However, what with helping her mother, doing the housework, rehearsing songs and performing six nights a week plus two matinées, her life was too full to spend all the time brooding. Whenever she thought of Ned, she tried not to think about wounds and battlefields, but of happier times to come.

Her favourite fantasy was to imagine their wedding. Oh,

how she was looking forward to that! She would walk proudly down the aisle looking just like Elizabeth had done, like an angel swathed in clouds of net and tulle and satin!

On her imaginary wedding day, Mrs Gates would be smiley and pleasant, Mr Gates would look every inch the noble, saintly invalid, Susannah would be the most beautiful bridesmaid in the world, Archie would toddle behind them as the pageboy, and – and here imagination really did take her over! – their best man would be none other than that rake and reprobate Phillip Gates, come back from Paris specially to perform his filial duty.

For some reason she pictured Phillip as fair as Ned was dark. Susannah had blonde hair, after all. Phillip would have steely grey eyes, aristocratic features and be deadly with a sword or a gun. He would be well read, able to quote from the classics, and be a follower of fashion whose critical eye for the perfect shoe or glove was second to none. She had no idea why Ned's rakish brother should intrigue her so. He just did.

When Christmas came and went without further word from Ned, Lily began to fret. Perhaps he had been injured and was lying in some awful, unhygienic field hospital, unable to write. If only she could go to him... But Africa was so far, thousands of miles away. There was nothing she could do but wait, along with so many other women.

At last three letters arrived together, tied up with red string. Their dates were quite widely spaced and Lily could only think that there had been a hold-up in the system somewhere and they had all caught up with one another. Like Ned's earlier missives, they didn't tell her much at all;

it was hot and dusty, he missed her, he wished he were back in England…

Once more, Lily felt cheated. She wanted vivid letters that would enable her to feel she were right there on the battlefield with him. She wanted to hear the snorts and whinnies of the horses, see their breath steaming in the chilly early morning air, hear the jangle of stirrups, the gleam of spurs and highly polished boots, hear the trumpets call, the men shout, the thunder of the horses' hooves. If Billy had been the soldier, rather than Ned, he could have described it all for her…

Then she reminded herself sternly that Billy still didn't know how to write. Anyway, how *dare* she think of spiteful, cruel Billy Morgan in the same breath as heroic Ned? The wording on the poster currently displayed outside the Old Mo floated into her mind. It said: *Tonight! Hear lovely Lavender Blue sing "My Heart Is With You, Soldier Lad", written by favourite songwriter Billy Morgan.* There they were, all three of them, mentioned in the same sentence – herself, her soldier lad, and Billy. Life certainly played some funny jokes on you sometimes, she thought wryly.

On January 15th, shortly before Lily was due on stage, Reggie, the backstage messenger, burst into Lily's dressing-room and announced that Mr Graydon needed to see her urgently in his office. This was so unusual and irregular that Lily experienced a cold stab of alarm. Had somebody complained about her act? Was he about to tell her to drop one of her songs? Or, even worse, was she about to hear the dreadful news that she was no longer required to sing on the stage of the Old Mo?

It was none of these – but it was far, far worse.

James Graydon's office door was open and he could be seen pacing back and forth. Lily swallowed nervously. "You wished to see me?" she enquired.

"Yes, yes, come in, my dear." He looked extremely ill at ease as he closed the door behind her and it was only then that Lily saw that there was a third person in the room who had been standing to one side of the door. Her brother, Harry.

It could only mean one thing! Her hand flew to her mouth. "Father!" she cried. Mother had always said that his excessive use of alcohol would kill him one day.

Harry walked over to her, his face grave, and took both her hands in his. "It's true that I've brought bad news, Lily. It happened several days ago but news has only just reached his family. They sent a letter…"

"Ned." Lily's head swam.

"Yes, Ned," Harry confirmed gently and his arms were there to support her as she sank down in an all-obliterating swoon.

"It's the shock…"

"He was her fiancé…"

"We'd better get her home…"

The words circled around her head like goldfish in an echoey bowl as Lily gradually came to. As her head cleared, the knowledge hit her like a rock. Ned was dead.

"H-how did he die?" she whispered, accepting the glass of water handed to her by Reggie. "Was it bravely in battle? Oh, I hope he didn't suffer!"

She was so busy dabbing her eyes with the handkerchief

170

supplied by Harry that she failed to notice the way her brother's lips momentarily tightened.

"Yes it was, and no, he didn't suffer," Harry assured her.

James Graydon was talking to Reggie, telling him to make an announcement between acts that Lavender Blue had suffered a tragic bereavement and wouldn't be appearing that evening.

Lily got up from the chair on which Harry had placed her. She pushed away his arm which was offered in support and shook her head, curling her toes in an attempt to stand up straight. "Of course I'm going on!" she insisted. "Ned would have wanted it. I must be brave, too. I shall sing in his memory."

The audience fell silent as Lily herself told them of the news that had just reached her.

"I want to dedicate this song to Ned Gates and to all the other brave men who have fallen while defending their land," she said in a tear-choked voice, as Joe played the opening bars of *My Heart Is With You, Soldier Lad*.

It was time to begin singing. She opened her mouth and only a whisper emerged – but what a whisper! It filled the hushed auditorium with a husky lament like the echo of a mournful ghost. Listeners held their breath as Lily's voice gradually swelled, rich and plaintive, giving the most honest, heart-rending performance of that song that they had ever heard.

When she reached the final, whispered, wistful repetition of "I'll kiss you in my dreams", a woman, maybe someone else who had lost a sweetheart in Africa, sobbed out loud. Lily walked to the front of the stage, a slight, pale figure, her long, dark hair cascading over her shoulders and down the bodice of her trademark lavender dress. Bending, she picked up her basket of dried lavender and took out one piece at a time, kissing it before tossing it into the audience. It was as if every sprig was a life carelessly tossed aside by battle. When she had emptied her basket, she put it down on the stage and launched into an unaccompanied version of *Lavender Blue*, her pure voice shot through with a throb of emotion.

When her act was finished, Lily felt completely drained. Her legs felt weak as she walked off stage. Frightened of fainting again, she reached out, trying to catch hold of the strut of a piece of scenery. She missed, and stumbled against someone who was walking towards her. Strong arms went round her and steadied her.

"Thank you," she gasped – then she saw who it was. "Billy! What are you doing backstage?"

"I met Harry in the street and he told me. I wanted to – well – tell you how very sorry I am. It's a dreadful thing to happen."

She knew he was being sincere. She *felt* it. It was in the serious set of his mouth, the compassion in his eyes. "Thank you for your sympathy, Billy," she told him.

"Well, if there's ever anything an old friend can do…"

"Thank you," she said again.

"It could have happened to anyone…"

Lily stared at him. Had he just gone mad? "What do you mean?" she asked, turning on him angrily. "Of course it couldn't!"

"Well, it could if you did a lot of riding or hunting."

Lily still had no idea what he was talking about. "Look, Billy Morgan, I've just heard news that my fiancé was killed in battle six days ago, and now you're rambling on about hunting. What's going on?"

It was Billy's turn to stare. "Killed in battle? Ned Gates wasn't killed in battle! What on earth gave you *that* idea? He was killed when his horse put its foot in a hole and fell on him. He was racing against a friend. They had a bet." Billy stopped, aware of Lily's dismayed eyes and ghastly pallor.

Lily raised her hand and struck Billy across the face. "How *dare* you tell such dreadful lies about a war hero?" she shrieked. "How could you be so cruel? Ned died in battle. I don't know where this lunatic story about a race came from. Ned wasn't a gambling man. He would never have ridden a dangerous race for a foolish bet. You've made it up and – and I wish I knew why!"

Lily broke down and started crying. Billy reached out, a look of tender concern on his face, but she violently shoved him away. "Get out of my sight," she hissed. "You're evil! I never want to see you again."

She sank to the wooden boards and sobbed until another pair of helpful arms appeared from somewhere and helped her to her feet. This time they belonged to Harry, who walked her slowly home and handed her over to their mother, who mixed her a soothing cordial and put her to bed. But she couldn't sleep. She spent half the night crying about Ned and the other half cursing Billy. How could he tell a pack of lies about a dead man to his grieving fiancée? What was he trying to prove? Maybe he was truly mad. She hoped he would heed her words and keep out of her way from now on.

Sometime during the following terrible day, Harry came in to see her as she lay prostrate in bed.

"H-how are you?" he asked nervously, as if expecting to get his head bitten off. But Lily felt too weak with grief to pick a fight with him.

"As well as can be expected," she replied. "Would you kindly mind telling me if you ran into Billy Morgan outside the theatre the other night?"

Harry nodded, then cleared his throat noisily. He looked both anxious and embarrassed.

"Did you tell him about ... about Ned? He says you did."

"Yes, I did," Harry confessed.

"And did you tell him exactly what you told me, about Ned having died heroically on the battlefield?"

A fiery crimson blush spread upwards from Harry's neck and suffused his face, and he stood awkwardly by the bed, unable – or unwilling – to reply.

"Answer me," Lily said. "What did you tell him?"

"The truth."

"And what, pray, is the truth? That Ned died a hero, or that he died in some foolish sounding escapade involving a bet and a race?"

Harry cleared his throat once more.

In a low, weak voice, Lily asked, "Please tell me. I want to know."

"No, you wouldn't want to know," Harry replied stubbornly and left the room, leaving Lily even more upset and confused. Now she didn't know what to believe, and she rolled on to her side, curled into a ball and cried until her mother came in to bathe her hot, salt-streaked face.

That was when Lily remembered something. "Mother, Harry said there was a letter. The letter from Ned's family, explaining how he died. I should like very much to see it, please."

"I'm not sure if it would be a good idea," her mother said dubiously. "I don't know if you're ready for it."

"Ned was my fiancé and I have every right to read that letter. In fact, it should have been given to me unopened!" Lily insisted.

"It wasn't addressed to you, it was addressed to us, your parents, as Mr and Mrs Gates thought it best that we should break the news to you."

"That was thoughtful of them!" remarked Lily scathingly.

"It *was*!" responded her mother. "Very thoughtful. They seem nice people."

"What? Nice? Mr and Mrs Gates? They totally disapproved of me. Ned said so!"

"I wouldn't believe everything Ned says … I mean, said," her mother stumbled.

Lily's brow knitted in a frown. Was everybody against her? Billy, Harry, and now her own mother? What was going on?

"Mother, if you don't let me see that letter, I shall ask Father, and if he won't give it to me, I shall hunt high and low until I find it. And if you've hidden it, or thrown it away, I shall rise from my bed now and travel all the way to Kingston-Upon-Thames to find out the truth!"

In reality, Lily could have hardly made it to Waterloo station in her weak state. She hadn't eaten for two days. However, her mother decided enough was enough and fetched her the letter, leaving the room and closing the door so that Lily could digest its contents in peace.

We are sorry to inform you of the loss in South Africa of our elder son, Ned. The news reached us today but apparently the accident occurred almost a week ago…

Accident? Lily's heart missed a beat. Billy's story couldn't be true … it couldn't! *Please let it be a lie*, she prayed. She read on and discovered almost instantly that her prayer had gone unheeded.

Ned had a very fine horse, Sultan, which we bought him ourselves. A fellow officer bet Ned that his horse, Kismet, could outrun Sultan. During the ensuing race, Sultan unfortunately put his foot in a hole and fell and Ned was crushed beneath him. He died instantly.

We are telling you these details so that you can decide yourselves whether to impart them to your daughter, or whether it would be better to convince her that Ned died a brave death on the battlefield. We sympathize with her grief at this time and hope that in time she will be able to come to terms with what has occurred. She is young and we wish her well and hope she will find happiness in the future.

Yours in sorrow, Lionel and Beatrice Gates.

Chapter 18

The notepaper fluttered from Lily's hand as she sank back against the pillows, her eyelids closed as she attempted to take in the facts outlined so baldly in the letter. So Billy's tale had been true and he hadn't known that Harry had followed the other path suggested by Mr and Mrs Gates, and had decided to shield her from the truth. She had been horrible to Billy, hitting him and screaming at him like that. Would he be able to understand that she herself was hardly in her right mind, having only just found out that Ned had been killed?

But she couldn't think about Billy now. There was too much else to take in. She started to feel sorry for Ned. Poor thing. What a horrible way to die! Billy had been right, being crushed by a horse could happen to any rider, if he or she were unfortunate enough not to be thrown clear when their mount fell. Then a sneaking anger started up inside her. Ned had obviously had time on his hands, if he could lark around idly like that. Why could he not have written her longer letters? Had bets and races meant more to him than the girl he loved? Then she promptly told herself off for thinking badly of him.

Her mother came back in and sat on the edge of Lily's bed. She reached for her daughter's clammy hand and stroked it comfortingly, the way she had done when Lily had been small and had awoken in terror from a nightmare. "I'm sorry you had to find out the truth," she said.

"It's all right. It's probably better that I should know," Lily murmured.

"You hadn't known him very long really, dear," her mother reminded her. "It would have been worse if it had happened *after* you were married."

One look at Lily's bleak expression told her that maybe she was on the point of saying too much. She smoothed back the hair from her daughter's flushed brow and left her to sleep – which at last Lily did.

The last person she expected to receive a visit from next day was Phillip Gates. Lily was lying dazedly in bed, not sure what time of day it was, her mind still haunted by pictures of a writhing horse and Ned's crushed body beneath it, when her mother tapped on the door, then came in.

"There's a young gentleman to see you, Lily," she said.

"If it's Billy, tell him I'm not ready to speak to anybody, particularly him," she replied. In her heart, she had partially forgiven him for being the bearer of bad tidings. It was Harry she should really be angry with – and yet he had only been doing what he thought best for her. There was far too much confusion around her, and only one solid fact: that Ned was dead.

"No, it's not Billy, it's Ned's brother, Phillip," was the surprising response.

Immediately, Lily sat bolt upright in bed. Two spots of colour flared in her pale cheeks as she hotly informed her mother, "That rake and scoundrel? How dare he come here! I will not see him on any account."

"He seems like a very pleasant young man," her mother said in his defence. "Very ordinary. Not in the slightest bit a rake. Have you ever actually met him?"

Lily frowned. "No, but Ned told me about him," she grunted. "Tell me, Mother, what is he here for?"

"He is in London to arrange a memorial service for his brother. He wishes to pay his respects to you. I really do think it is only polite to see him," her mother insisted.

Lily gave in. "Five minutes," she declared frostily. "That is all he can have of my time. I shall get up. Please ask him to wait."

When Lily reluctantly entered the small, cramped living-room, her eyes went immediately to the young man who was standing quietly by the dresser. At once, she felt puzzled. Surely this small, plump, mousy-looking man with the thick, round spectacles couldn't be rake-hell Phillip, the scourge of Parisian gambling saloons and bawdy houses?

"Please allow me to introduce myself," he said.

Lily tentatively extended a cold hand and felt it squeezed briefly by Phillip's warm one.

"Phillip tells me he had to leave his studies at the Sorbonne just before his examinations, in order to make the arrangements for the memorial service for Ned," Cecily explained. Ned's remains had already been laid to rest in a military cemetery in South Africa.

"Oh," said Lily. She looked at Phillip. "So you're a student?"

"Yes, that's right," he confirmed, with a shy smile. Apart from his spectacles, she could see that, with his warm,

179

ready smile and honey-gold curls, he quite resembled his sister, Susannah, and didn't look a bit like his dark, broody-looking brother.

"Ned told me that you were a gambler who lived a wild life in Paris." The words tumbled from Lily's mouth before she could consider the wisdom of saying them.

"A gambler? Wild life? *Me?*" To Lily's amazement, despite the fact that Phillip was wearing the black armband of mourning, he burst into peals of laughter.

"Pray tell me what I have said that's so amusing?" Lily asked stiltedly. She felt a little dizzy, as if the world that she knew was tilting this way and that, and upside-down.

"Ned assured me that you had been banished by the family for your unforgivable behaviour, and I have no reason to believe that he told a lie. And why should he? Ned was a fine, upstanding man. He may have had some friends amongst his regiment whose standards weren't quite as high as his own, but he was different. I certainly never knew him to gamble, or get drunk, or frequent certain dubious establishments, all the things he said you did, although I must say that the evidence of my own eyes would lead me to think otherwise..."

"The evidence of your own eyes is correct!" Phillip said angrily. "I know one shouldn't speak ill of the dead, but that's typical of my brother, blaming others for his own vices!"

"I only know what Ned told me," Lily said dully. She really didn't know what was going on at all.

Sensing the tension, Lily's mother broke it by announcing that she would go and make tea for them both. ·

"I know he was my brother, but I hated him," Phillip

said, as soon as Cecily had gone, as if thinking Lily's mother might disapprove of such an anti-family statement. He bit his lip and his eyelids flickered as he glanced downwards at his feet.

Then he raised his eyes again and gazed candidly at Lily. "I'm sorry to have to say this, but Ned was a coward, a liar and a bully. Because I was smaller and weaker than him, and had poor eyesight, he used to pick on me. I lost count of the amount of pinches, punches and kicks I received from him. I was always black and blue. Susannah will tell you, if you care to ask her."

Lily recalled a couple of occasions when Ned had gripped her painfully tight, and hurt her. "Why are you telling me all this?" she asked.

"Because knowing the truth might make your period of mourning easier. I discussed it with Mother. She agreed that it was better you should know. When Ned first spoke about his plans to marry a music-hall singer, we thought ... well, that you would be the sort of girl who was no better than she should be. But when Ned brought you home, they realized that you were an *ingénue*."

"What does that mean?" Lily asked suspiciously.

"It means natural and unspoiled and without artifice. The fact that my sister took to you straight away was proof enough. She has a good instinct for people. And my father is a good judge of character. He has to be, in his business. 'Perhaps our Ned is improving with age,' Father said after he had met you. 'Lily isn't one of his usual floozies.'"

"So he usually mixed with 'floozies', did he?" Lily enquired.

Phillip didn't answer, but the way he raised his eyebrows

181

was comment enough. "Don't take this wrong, Lily," he said, "but Father and Mother both wondered what it was about you that attracted Ned. All his other lady friends had been older and more experienced than you. Many were divorced, some still married. Ned didn't care, so long as they had money to lavish on him. Father decided that he saw you as a long-term investment, someone who would be willing to tread the boards for ever, a source of cash that would never run out, thus allowing him to lead a carefree, idle life. He hoped to ensnare you young, while you were besotted with him and still naïve enough not to see him for what he was…"

Lily felt a lump in her throat. She still felt very confused, as well she might be, seeing that Phillip's words had turned her vision of Ned the hero upside-down.

"Wh-why should I believe you?" she said shakily. "How do I know that you're telling me the truth?" It was the last gasp of her old love for Ned talking. In her heart, she already felt that the picture Phillip was painting was the true one, but still, she didn't quite want to believe it.

"When it became obvious that I was destined for university, I begged Father to send me to Paris, to study at the Sorbonne, simply to get away from Ned. I was sick of his bullying, and having my allowance stolen by him to pay for his bad habits. Yes, at sixteen he was already frequenting drinking and gambling dens. He was running wild. Father couldn't do anything about it.

"Once I was in Paris, Father used to write me regular letters in which he was at his wits' end about Ned's latest escapades. I brought one of them with me, thinking that you might indeed demand proof."

Phillip slipped the letter out of the inside pocket of his jacket and handed it to Lily, waiting in silence while she read it. During this time, Cecily brought in the tea then, seeing how absorbed the two young people were, tiptoed discreetly out again and could be heard clattering pots in the kitchen.

The letter was postmarked with a date in the April of two years previously and contained a long list of complaints about Ned. Its tone was one of utter despair. Lily read it through twice, then handed it back to Phillip. She felt quite drained by it. "I believe you now," she said. "How could he behave so callously, with so little regard for you all?"

"His behaviour nearly killed Father," Phillip went on. "He was having to use his own money to pay off Ned's gambling debts and couldn't send me any allowance to help pay for my studies. It meant that I had to find menial work behind the bar of an artists' café in Montmartre. Mother managed to keep the family jewels from him, but only just, otherwise Ned would have sold those, too."

The ruby engagement ring, thought Lily. Maybe Ned had planned to sell the real jewel and get a fake made to give to her, knowing that she would never know the difference. What a gullible little fool she had been! Maybe she should have listened to the likes of Sweet Jennie Brown and Flora Brock, after all.

"I'm sorry that you aren't to be my sister-in-law after all, but, if I may say so, I'm glad, too," Phillip concluded. "My brother would never have brought you happiness. He would have crushed your spirit like he crushed mine. He would have got his hand on every penny of your earnings to feed his gambling habit. And not only that…"

He paused and glanced awkwardly at Lily, as if unsure whether to continue.

"Go on," she encouraged quietly.

He lowered his voice and spoke hurriedly. "He would never have been faithful to you. Ned was incapable of being faithful to anybody. He used to write me letters boasting about his successes with ladies, even – and I'm sorry to have to tell you this, Lily – even after he had met you."

"Oh!" Lily gasped in shock and raised her hand to her face. She felt her stomach churn. Then, in her confusion, she rose and began pouring tea with a shaky hand, splashing it on to the cloth. Her heart was thudding. She hadn't known Ned at all, she realized. She had only known the charming mask he had worn to hide the disreputable person he really was. For she believed Phillip implicitly. He had honest eyes, he was incapable of lying.

Phillip took a step towards her, as if prepared to catch her if she were about to faint. "I'm sorry, Lily. Maybe I shouldn't have…?" he faltered, stepping back again.

Lily shook her head. "It's all right," she mumbled. "I … well, I need some time to take it in."

Phillip nodded. "I'm sorry this has all been such a shock to you. I think maybe I had better go now. Goodbye, Lily."

He held out his hand and Lily took it. "Goodbye, Phillip. And thank you. This can't have been easy for you."

His rueful smile told her she was right.

"Good luck with your studies," she said.

She and her mother showed him out. As soon as he had gone, Lily flung herself on her bed and heaved dry, racking, angry, tearing sobs. Handsome, lying Ned. She had been thoroughly taken in by him. Now, the grief that she felt was for herself and all the time she had wasted thinking herself so in love with him. It felt like a wound that would never heal.

She would never marry now, she decided: never give her heart again. She would never be able to trust her own judgement and couldn't risk falling all over again for another plausible cheat with a handsome face. No, there was only one thing for her now and that was her career. She would work at being the greatest music-hall singer the world had ever known. *Move over, Marie Lloyd,* she thought determinedly: *your time is up!*

Chapter 19

Mr Graydon had insisted on Lily taking two weeks off to recover from her tragedy. She would hardly be able to entertain an audience, make them laugh at her humorous songs, if her heart was heavy as lead, he said.

Perhaps two weeks weren't long enough, for Lily found she couldn't shake off the hollow, dragging feeling of grief and disappointment. She had expected it to vanish the moment she stepped back on stage, full of her new determination to work at being the best music-hall star of all time, but it didn't. She could hear her voice coming out thin and weak, was aware of her audience staring at her, puzzled, wondering what was wrong.

She took a deep breath, filling her lungs with air, and tried again. She had always thought singing was easy – you just took a breath, opened your mouth and the sound came out. This weedy, reedy voice wasn't hers at all. She'd never heard it before. It was as if a stranger had crept inside her vocal cords and replaced her loud, sweet voice with this … this mockery.

My Heart Is With You, Soldier Lad was more popular than ever, with so many men fighting the Boers. Lily started the song determined to wrench every scrap of meaning from it and rend every heartstring. But it didn't work. She had no sooner begun than her vision of a proud soldier marching towards the enemy was replaced by one of Ned tumbling ignominiously off his horse as the result of a drunken bet, not an enemy rifle.

She faltered, her memory dried, she forgot the lyrics, halted, tried again, made a few words up and somehow stumbled through to the end. But, even before Joe had stopped playing the final bars, the audience began to jeer and boo and hiss. It was the first time that Lily had ever faced a hostile audience, though music-hall audiences were notorious for booing performers that they didn't like. Even on her very first night, when she had been terrified, they had treated her kindly. They should be treating her kindly now. Surely they had all heard about her fiancé being killed? And none of them knew the real reason.

She hesitated, unsure of what to do. "My friends…" she began. The volume of the jeers increased and mocking laughter swelled from the rows of seats. Friends? They weren't her friends. They were the enemy, as surely as the Boers were the enemy of those brave soldiers on the front line.

Bursting into tears, she ran from the stage and stumbled sobbing towards her dressing-room. A familiar, hated voice penetrated her thoughts. "So! Got your come-uppance at last, did you? Good. You had it coming for a long time. Now perhaps you'll return to the gutter you crawled out of and leave the stage to *experienced* performers like ourselves!"

She looked up into the sneering faces of Sweet Jennie Brown and her sidekick, the horrible Flora Brock, who had made up Lily's face so revoltingly on the night of her first ever performance at the Old Mo.

"I must say I miss that Sergeant Gates – don't you, Jennie?" Flora rolled her blue painted eyelids at her friend. "Such good company. So *generous!*" She left Lily in no doubt as to her meaning.

Lily leapt to her feet and gave Flora a push. "Get away from me!" she screeched. "You horrible, horrible women! It's you who should be crawling back into the gutter, you … *SLIME!*"

Racked with anguish, Lily ran down the backstage passages, ran and ran until she pushed through an exit door and found herself out on the frosty street. She had left her coat and hat in the dressing-room, but she wasn't going back for them now. She would collect them in the morning, when she came to deliver the note to Mr Graydon telling him that she was never going to sing again.

Her ambitions to be a great music-hall artiste and to buy a wonderful house for her family were over. She didn't have the stage in her blood. She was, after all, only a working-class girl and she should be content with a job such as Harry's Ellen had, in a nice, quiet shop with nobody to taunt her. Set yourself up as a star, and you set yourself up to be knocked down, she could see that perfectly now. What she needed was a small, dark, silent place to crawl into and hibernate until she started feeling better. Fortunately, she had her savings. They should last for quite a time…

"Mother, teach me how to hem-stitch," Lily requested. After three weeks away from the stage, she was getting bored.

"I tried to teach you when you were small. You were the

most cack-handed person with a needle that I had ever seen," her mother pointed out.

"Give me another try. I'd like to learn to help you."

"Here…" Cecily showed her exactly how to angle the needle and how to catch up just enough material to hold the hem, but not so much as to show the stitch on the other side.

Lily practised and practised and in the end, with an impatient sigh, she banged the piece of scrap material she was using down on the table. "I may as well give up," she snorted.

"Told you!" laughed her mother. "You're not cut out to be a seamstress. You never were."

"Not 'cut out', indeed! Did you intend that as a pun, Mother?"

"No, I didn't. Good one though, isn't it? Look, Archie's laughing, too." Cecily glanced towards the window, which was open to let some of the fresh March air in. "It's a lovely afternoon. Why don't you take the lad out for a breath of fresh air? Put the reins on him so he won't dash into the road. You know how he loves horses."

It was true. Archie went into raptures every time he saw a horse. "Horsey, horsey!" he would yell, and would try his best to reach the huge animal and pat the only part he could reach, its legs. They all lived in fear of Archie receiving a fatal kick one of these days, which was why his mother had hit on the idea of making him wear a set of reins designed specially for toddlers. They had bells on them so that as he ran, he jingled. He loved his blue leather reins and would prance and toss his head, pretending to be a horse.

In this fashion, Archie cantered down Long Acre with a laughing Lily in tow. They turned down Bow Street and then went over Waterloo Bridge where Lily paused to take in the breathtaking sight of the gracious dome of St Paul's rising above the splendid new office buildings which had been built alongside the Thames. A barge passed beneath the bridge, leaving a vee-shape of sparkling water. A seagull mewed overhead. Lily lifted her face to the wind. There was a hint of warmth in it. Soon, it would be properly spring – but how different from last spring! No music, no Ned... Last year had held so much promise, but what did she have to look forward to now?

"Lily, Lily! Wanna go home!" Archie complained, his small feet tired from thumping the hard pavement.

"Come along, then," Lily said, feeling like a nursemaid. The thought suddenly struck her that perhaps this was a job she could do – look after children. She had a knack of being able to enter into their world and their thoughts. She saw herself in a nurse's uniform, pushing a posh pram around Hyde Park and stopping to gossip with the other girls. They would sit on a bench with the perambulators parked in front, where they could keep an eye on them, and they would talk wickedly about their employers, bemoan the bad habits of their small charges, giggle about young men who had caught their fancy...

And I would be the odd one out, thought Lily wryly. There would be no more young men for her. She was never going to be fooled like that again. It was much too risky. Just imagine tying yourself for ever to a man who turned out to be quite the opposite to the man he seemed, having put on an act to catch you! She would soon be eighteen. Any girl who was at all attractive had a sweetheart by the age of eighteen. If not, she risked being left on the shelf. But Lily had voluntarily climbed on to the highest shelf of all and she wanted to be left there in the darkest corner at the very back of the marriage shop for ever!

Dusk was drawing in as they reached home. Cecily had put away her dressmaking for the day and was concentrating instead on making a stew with steak and onions, cabbage, carrots and potatoes. It smelt delicious.

"I'll go and change Archie," Lily volunteered.

She was just unwrapping the kicking toddler from his bundle of clothes when the strains of accordion music reached her ears. It was quite loud and sounded as if it were coming from somewhere close to their house – drifting through next door's window, perhaps. Accordion music was very popular. Many people could play the squeeze-box, but this player was particularly skilled, and the tune, though she didn't know it, was very beautiful. After divesting Archie of his tight jacket and outdoor leggings, and removing his wet napkin, she opened the living-room window and peered out into the gathering twilight.

The player was standing directly outside their house. His face was turned up towards her window and her heart leapt as she recognized Billy. Swiftly, she ducked behind the curtain, her face flaming as she remembered how she had hit him and shouted at him when he had told her the true circumstances of Ned's death. Then, she had thought he was cruelly taunting her, though now she realized that he had been speaking in all innocence, thinking Harry had already told her. She owed him a massive apology – one so big that the words for it didn't exist.

Why was he here now, playing such haunting music? Perhaps now, having had so long to ponder her treatment of him, he had decided that he really would taunt her with these romantic strains to remind her of the love she had lost; that false, empty love. Oh, surely not even Billy Morgan could be that cruel?

Had Billy ever been really unkind to her? He had made some pointed jibes when he had learned of her relationship with Ned – but then, like other people, perhaps he had assumed that she knew the truth about him, and had chosen to associate with him in spite of them, thus going down in his estimation.

Tears stung her eyes. The music was still wafting in through the window, strains which seemed to pluck every emotional nerve in her body. *Stop it, stop it, Billy, before you drive me mad!* she thought, and flung the window wide.

His face lifted up to her. "Hello, Lily," he said.

Wordlessly, she stared down at him, her heart performing some strange dance that was not at all in time with the music. She was glad to see him. So glad. But she could never tell him, because she had no right at all to feel this way, after treating him so badly.

She had to say she was sorry. That was the only thing she could do. Maybe that was why he was here; what he was waiting for.

"Come down, Lily, I want to talk to you," he said gently, as if trying not to scare a nervous animal.

"Are you sure you want to, after last time?" she asked dubiously.

"Yes, sure," he echoed.

"Then I'll come."

"Mother, Billy Morgan's at the door. I'm just going down to see him," she told her mother as she passed through the kitchen.

"Billy *who*?" her mother asked, but Lily had already vanished.

A wave of shyness overcame her as soon as she saw him. He was wearing a jacket of damson velvet, and smart grey trousers. His hair had been tamed by a recent haircut and he looked extremely smart and handsome, far too smart to be a busker.

Billy rested his accordion end-up on the corner of the step and held out his hand to her.

Lily shook her head and clasped both of hers behind her back. He gave her a puzzled look. She stared down at her feet, dumb with shame.

"Speak to me, Lily…" he urged.

She shook her head again. She was willing herself to say "Sorry," but despite forming the word on her tongue several times, she couldn't get her vocal cords to give it sound.

His hand crept behind her, unfastened one of her tightly clasped ones and held it in a warm, reassuring grip. Little tingles began to dance up her arm.

She opened her mouth. "I … I…" she stammered.

"What is it? Come on, it's not a copper, it's your old friend Billy!" He laughed. It was a sympathetic sound, not a taunting one. She tried again.

"Billy, I … I'm sorry."

There! She'd said it at last. A great weight dropped from her. She blinked her eyes twice, then opened them wide. Billy was smiling.

"You've nothing to say 'sorry' for," he said. "It was my fault. I thought you already knew. I met Harry next day and he explained. So it is I who should be saying 'sorry'."

They stared at each other in silence, Lily feeling as if birds were fluttering their wings inside her. Not smoky grey London pigeons, but doves. White doves against a blue sky. She was floating away.

Billy squeezed her hand, anchoring her again.

"How … how is your songwriting going?" she asked him awkwardly, trying to ignore the effect that his eyes were having on her. He seemed so tall – taller than Ned, taller than Harry. He made her feel small and delicate and feminine. She felt herself going all weak and melty. He was absolutely gorgeous – but he was Billy Morgan, she reminded herself. Billy, whom she had known for years. Billy, who had rejected her on that long-ago occasion on the boat, when he had refused to kiss her.

But had he even known that she had wanted his kiss and expected it? Maybe he had feared to kiss her in case she had thought him too fresh and forward! After all, they had always been like brother and sister. Maybe even now he still thought of her as a sister, or an old friend, and didn't see her as a woman. So that sparkle in his eye wasn't meant as a sign of appreciation for her feminine beauty, it was simply the sparkle of his high spirits and love of life in general. There was nothing personal in it at all.

She turned her attention to what Billy was telling her about his successes with various songs. It seemed that he was making quite a lot of money from his music.

"I've bought my own houseboat," he told her excitedly. "It's not very big, but it's moored at Blackfriars."

"I'd love to see it!" Lily heard herself saying, then promptly told herself off for sounding too eager.

"And I'd love you to see it. Why not come tomorrow?" he invited her.

Recklessness surged through her. Why not? "Morning or afternoon?" she asked him breathlessly.

"Morning would be best," he replied.

"I'll see if Mother can spare me..."

Of course Cecily could. In fact, she was only too pleased to see her daughter looking animated again and more like her old self.

"It's only Billy," Lily reassured her next morning. "He's just an old friend. He wrote some of the songs I used to sing."

Her mother gave her a knowing look, but decided not to tease her. "Get along with you," she urged. "It's a fine morning for a walk. And if you're going to be back by lunch-time, bring me some nice, thin-sliced ham from the butcher's, would you?"

"Of *course* I'll be back by lunch-time!" Lily prophesied. "What on earth would I find to talk to Billy about for three hours?" It was only twenty past nine!

Starlings shrieked raucously from chimney-pots as she made her way along Endell Street and down Bow Street, heading for the Aldwych. It was cold but exhilarating. Lily lifted her face to the March wind. Its icy needles pin-pricked her face and lifted her hair. Her wind-whipped eyes watered. She hadn't felt so alive in ages. Her pace quickened. She couldn't wait to get to Billy's boat, yet she didn't know why. She felt like running, skipping and jumping and throwing out her arms.

Here was the Thames, a glittering silver swell. Lily descended the steps by Waterloo Bridge and started walking east, towards St Paul's. Boats bobbed on the water, tugging at their mooring ropes. Billy's boat was called the *Anna Leyden*. It was a Dutch barge which had been converted to a houseboat. It was easy to find, moored by one of the many wooden landing stages that projected from both banks into the river. "It's two pontoons down from the Fire Brigade," Billy had told her.

The London Fire Brigade had a floating fire station near Blackfriars Bridge. In the summer, a wonderful garden was planted on it and the masses of colourful flowers were admired by all who walked over the bridge. Right now, every box and tub was full of bright daffodils, their sunshine yellow heads nodding in the stiff breeze that blew up the river.

The wooden landing stage was slippery and Lily made her way gingerly to the end, where the *Anna Leyden* was moored. She was a smart boat, painted black and red with her name picked out in gold.

"Billy!" Lily called. "It's Lily."

A hatch opened and Billy popped his head out. He grinned and climbed right out on the deck. "I'll just bring her closer in, then you can come aboard," he said.

He pulled on the mooring rope until the boat bumped against the landing stage's supporting struts. As the tide was low, the deck was about four feet below her. Lily regarded it dubiously, not seeing how she could possibly clamber on to the deck without breaking a leg.

"Jump. I'll catch you," Billy promised.

Lily knew that if she dithered, she would never do it.

She jumped. Time was suspended for a moment. She felt cold air rushing past her, snagging her skirts – and then she hit a yielding object and she and Billy crashed on to the deck together.

"Are you all right?" he asked, panting and laughing.

"Yes, I think so," she said, aware that her skirts had rucked up and she was showing far too much leg.

Billy stood up and held out a hand to her, pulling her to her feet. "Welcome to the *Anna Leyden*," he said. "I think you'll find her an improvement on my last boat."

"Oh, I thought the old one was rather…" She stopped, aware that if she continued, she might be giving herself away.

"Rather what?" he queried.

"Oh, nothing. It wasn't bad. I quite liked it, but there wasn't much room on it." *That was precisely what I liked about it – that it was so small that Billy and I had to sit really close together*, she thought.

"I think you'll find the *Anna* just as cosy," Billy said, and Lily felt her breath catch in her chest. Her heart hammered as she made her way carefully down the steep wooden steps into the cabin, holding her hem in one hand to prevent herself from tripping.

When she arrived in Billy's domain, she was surprised at the orderliness she found. A wooden table and bench stood over at one side and a stove glowed in the centre of the cabin, making so much heat that Lily couldn't wait to tug off her coat. A screen half hid a bunk, the covers of which had been smoothed and tucked in without a crease. A vase of dried flowers stood on the table. The air was sweet with an odour which was old-fashioned and very familiar.

"Lavender!" she exclaimed.

Billy's grin was a bit sheepish as he regarded the vase. "Yes, lavender," he confirmed.

Silence fell between them as colour flared and ebbed in Lily's cheeks. Lavender ... Lavender Blue. Was it intentional, or accidental?

"Did you get it ... for me?" she asked him.

Billy cast his eyes down. When he raised his head, his face was scarlet, yet he looked her bravely in the eye. "Not exactly *for* you, more because of you," he admitted. "I've always tried to keep some lavender on my boats."

"Because it makes the air smell nice?" It was an inane thing to say, but it was all she could think of saying with her heart leaping about inside her chest like a jack-in-the-box.

"Yes, that too, but mostly because it made me feel close to you. There. I didn't mean to say that. I'll shut up now and make us some tea." Billy rose and turned his back on her as he reached for the tea caddy on the shelf.

"Did you want to, then? Feel close to me? In spite of Ned and everything?"

Billy turned back again at the sound of Lily's voice.

"I never knew," she went on, in quiet wonder. "I never guessed. I thought you hated me!"

"Oh, Lily!" Billy dropped to his knees in front of the bench where Lily sat, and took her hands in his. "Oh, Lily," he said again. "If I seemed as if I hated you, it was only because I loved you so much. I was afraid."

"What were you afraid of?" Lily murmured, scarcely able to speak. Something was happening to her, something so enormous that she could feel the whole world expanding around her. There were rushing sounds in her ears.

198

A star-burst, an exploding sun – something was fizzing inside her, bursting out of her. She was turning inside out. She was lighter than air, she was floating. Floating towards Billy. Or was he pulling her towards him? Towards his lips?

"I thought you were too good for me. You could read and write, you sang like an angel, you had audiences eating out of your hand. You could have had any man you wanted to be your beau. I never thought you could ever want me," he said in a husky whisper. "I didn't think you could ever love me. But now I think – I *hope!* – that perhaps I was wrong."

A warm, dry brush of lip on lip. An opening, a melting, a clinging, a pouring of one soul into another's heart and a receiving of a soul in return. Lily had never suspected that a kiss could be like this. Compared to Billy's kisses, Ned's remembered ones seemed like a hollow charade, nothing but a painful pressure that had threatened to dislodge her teeth. Call that passion? It had only been empty posturing. *This* – this was real, inflaming every bit of her from her toes to the ends of her long, dark hair.

She was dizzy with happiness. She was dying from it. She wanted to die now, in Billy's arms, pressed so close to his chest that not even a sheet of music could fit between them. Oh, how wrong she had been to think she loved Ned! What an innocent child! To think she could have married him, not knowing what real love was – the bliss, the incredible, crazy, ecstatic happiness.

She began to laugh. The more she tried to stop herself, the more uncontrollable her laughter got. Billy pulled away from her and stared at her with a worried expression, that only made her laugh more.

"What is it, Lily? Have I said something wrong?" he said in a hurt tone.

"No … no," she gasped. "You've said something right. Absolutely right."

"What?" he murmured, placing his lips close to her ear. His breath on her sensitive skin made her shiver with delight. "What have I said that was right? Please tell me, Lily."

"That you hoped I could love you. Of course I can. I *do*! I think I always have done, right from when we very first met."

This time their kiss was different, full of hunger and need. All those lonely months when Billy had had to live with the jealous torture of knowing that Lily was due to marry Ned throbbed painfully in his kiss as he twisted and turned his head, searching, gasping, moaning, almost weeping. And Lily followed his kiss, tracing its source, feeling guilt and sympathy and grief and desire in turn, until at last her lips faltered and her head fell weakly on to Billy's shoulder.

For a while, he held her, stroking her hair. And then he said, "Well, Lily, where do we go from here?"

Lily answered, "I don't know," but in her heart she did. Her vow never to marry was dissolving like a spoonful of sugar thrown into the Thames on a warm day. She had feared being taken in by another Ned. But Billy wasn't a Ned. Billy was somebody she had known for a long time, someone who had never cheated or lied. Someone she herself had misjudged and hurt. She would never make that mistake again. She knew, as surely as she knew that the Thames would never stop flowing to the sea, that Billy was somebody she could trust with her life. Billy and she were going to be partners, in every sense of the word. Partners in life, in music, and in love.

Epilogue

TONIGHT! SERENADE YOUR EARS TO THE
STRAINS OF OUR SWEET SONGSTRESS, THE
LOVELY LAVENDER BLUE, SINGING THE SONGS
OF BILLY MORGAN, ACCOMPANIED BY BILLY HIM-
SELF WITH HARMONIES AND ACCORDION. THIS
NEW DOUBLE ACT SHOULD NOT BE MISSED!

The message was printed in huge black letters rimmed
with scarlet, on a yellow poster pasted outside the Old Mo.
Billy squeezed Lily's hand as they gazed at it.

"That's us, *cariad*, that's us!" he said in awe, his accent
sounding more Welsh than usual, like it always did at
emotional moments.

They had talked a lot, confessed a lot, planned a lot
since that day on the boat. Billy had told Lily of how he
had longed to comfort her after Ned's death, but had felt
that he had made such a mess of things that he hadn't
dared to come near her.

When he heard about her getting booed off the stage, he
had felt like throttling every member of the audience and
setting fire to the theatre. "How I ached for you," he said. "I
know how it feels. I was once pelted with rotten Brussels
sprouts by a crowd of cockneys for singing a song in Welsh."

"What did you do?" asked Lily, flinching at the thought of the humiliation he must have gone through.

"Sang another song in Welsh!" he said with a grin.

One of the conclusions they had come to on the boat was that together, they could face any audience, anywhere. They had met the next day and tried some of their old songs together – and if Lily's voice faltered just a little, a kiss from Billy made it strong again.

When they felt they had practised enough songs to have a proper act – difficult though it was to force themselves to sing, not to kiss – they went together to see James Graydon. When he heard them, he was bowled over and was only too pleased to give them a try-out as a duo. Tonight was to be their first performance.

"Pity you got to be known as Lavender Blue," Billy said. "Billy and Lily sounds perfect."

"It sounds perfect to me, too," Lily murmured, cuddling up to him as they stood there, gazing at their pictures on the poster.

"Everyone knows you as Lavender Blue, though. You can't change your name now," Billy pointed out.

"Oh yes, I can!" Lily's eyes danced as she imagined Billy's reaction to what she was about to say.

"What do you mean?" he wanted to know.

"I can change it to Lily Morgan," she said softly.

His face a study in surprised delight, Billy's dark eyes glowed into hers, as she had known they would.

"Would you...?" he breathed tenderly.

"Yes. One day. When you ask me," she replied, unaware that across the street a portly figure in a lavender waistcoat and grey bowler hat was smiling his approval at seeing the boy and girl he had marked out as born for each other, standing there hand in hand, together at last.

LAVENDER BLUE

Lavender's blue, diddle, diddle*
Lavender's green,
When I am king, diddle, diddle
You shall be queen.

Call up your men, diddle, diddle,
Set them to work,
Some to the plough, diddle, diddle,
Some to the cart.

Some to make hay, diddle, diddle,
Some to thresh corn,
Whilst you and I, diddle, diddle,
Keep ourselves warm.

*Nowadays, we are more familiar with the words, "Lavender's blue, dilly, dilly", but the original refrain was "diddle, diddle". It was changed to "dilly, dilly" in the 1940s when the old nursery rhyme was rearranged and recorded as a dance tune.

Historical Note

James Laurie Graydon was a real person. He was the manager of the New Middlesex Music Hall from 1871–1911 and was, by all accounts, a kindly and generous man who was much loved by everyone who knew him or worked for him. He was so concerned that his girl typists weren't getting enough to eat that he built a staff dining-room at the theatre, and at Christmas he gave food hampers to all the poor in the Covent Garden area. Graydon gave many famous music-hall stars their first break, including George Roby and Katie Lawrence, and Marie Lloyd sang at the New Middlesex when she was just starting out.

Look out for other new titles in the Forget Me Not series

The Wildest Dream

The shoot ended, the guests left and the castle lapsed into its normal routine. Lady Roscawl took to her bed, complaining of exhaustion after all the work she had done to entertain the visitors. Still confined indoors, Elizabeth spent most of her time in the library reading or pacing the corridors to try to work off some of her energy.

"You're going to marry a mummy's boy, I hear," William said to her one day. It was the first time that he had spoken to her for weeks.

Elizabeth did not reply, she just glared at him.

"At least we'll be rid of you."

"Go to hell, William." She had never sworn before, but she could not help herself.

"You're the one who's heading that way, Elizabeth."

From the look in his eyes, she knew that he was enjoying taunting her. She ignored his last remark and went up to her room, slamming the door behind her. He could not follow her there.

If only he knew that she planned to run away with Michael, that her wedding to Edward Cavendish would never take place. The only trouble was that Elizabeth hated deceit; she hated pretence of any sort, although she knew that she did not have any choice.

Thinking back to the spring, she remembered Sarah's wedding. Lord Homerton and her father were friends and colleagues at the House of Lords; she supposed they had worked out the match between them. Certainly Sarah had never laid eyes upon Johnny Homerton before he turned up at a shoot, but the difference was that she had liked him instantly. Sarah wanted to get married so that she could take her place in society; unlike Elizabeth, she did not question her way of life.

For a while, Elizabeth wondered what Sarah would have done if she had not liked Johnny, but she could not imagine her sister going against the wishes of her parents. She was glad that her sister's marriage seemed to be a happy one.

The weather had changed; a soft rain was falling. She went to the window and looked down to the stable yard and then beyond that to the rolling hills. A mile or two away, Michael would be hard at work on the roads. The thought of him brought a smile to her face; it would not be so long now.

A line of girls walked out of the yard, taking the track towards the village. Each of them was carrying a sack; they looked unhappy, though Elizabeth did not know why. Now that the shoot was over, the girls who had been taken on to help had been discharged. She thought they would have been glad of the chance of even a little work.

Eithne came in with a bundle of freshly laundered underwear, which she began to put away in a chest of drawers.

"The girls looked upset," Elizabeth said.

"Aye, Miss Elizabeth. They're not too pleased because they got paid in kind."

"What's that?"

"They got paid in meal and some cheese instead of money."

"What about the beaters? Did they get paid in meal as well?"

"I don't know. I suppose so."

Elizabeth's heart sank. She knew that Michael had been relying on money from the shoot to pay his fare to Liverpool. Eithne caught the look on her face.

"Is there anything the matter, Miss Elizabeth?"

"No," she said quickly. She did not want to burden the maid with her troubles, though she needed to get a message to Michael. "Could you ask Jamie to take a message to the village, Eithne?"

The maid had finished putting the underwear away. She stood up. "Jamie's gone, Miss Elizabeth. I thought you knew."

"Gone. Why?"

"He got the sack. They blamed him for letting you take the cart to the village."

The knowledge shot a bolt of guilt through Elizabeth.

"Don't worry," Eithne said, "he's a bright lad. He'll manage, if anyone can."

Although Elizabeth smiled, she felt pain inside. She had wanted to do good, but all she had done was to cause harm.

Lunch was an uncomfortable meal. Lady Roscawl was still in bed, and Elizabeth's brothers and father talked about estate matters as if she was not there. Once, she tried to join the conversation with a comment, but they ignored her, acting as if she had not spoken. Afterwards, she went to the library, where she began to flick through a copy of *Punch*; the cartoons always amused her.

Heavy footsteps disturbed her a short while later. The door was slightly ajar; she looked up and saw the factor pass by on his way to her father's study. Elizabeth waited for a moment, then she got up and followed him.

Carefully, she looked around, but there was nobody to see her. Raucous laughter came from the smoking-room, where her brothers were playing cards. Like a mouse, she crept along the corridor until she was outside the study.

Listening through the door, Elizabeth heard them talking about the shoot. Her father thanked Fraser for making sure it had gone so smoothly. The bag had been excellent. They chatted jovially for a while then, to end the conversation, her father said that he trusted that there were no problems.

"There is just one small thing," Fraser said. "I've decided to evict a tenant from Roscawl."

"Why's that? I thought the rents were paid."

"The rents are paid, right enough, but there's still arrears outstanding. There's one lad who's been causing a bit of trouble. I think we're best to get rid of him."

"Trouble? What kind of trouble? I thought that Young Ireland nonsense was over. I won't tolerate any of that on the estate."

"It's not that, Milord. No, this lad, O'Shea's his name, he set out to waylay a merchant by the name of O'Callaghan, would have robbed him but fortunately O'Callaghan's men were able to defend him. He's a troublemaker for sure. You're best to be rid of him. Besides, an eviction will keep the rest of them in line."

"Very well, Fraser. I'll leave it up to you," her father said.

Elizabeth slipped away, fear gnawing at the pit of her stomach. Michael had not tried to rob O'Callaghan, he had simply tried to get a fair price for the oats; he had told her all about it. She had to get word to him quickly, warn him what was going on.

Then, with sickening certainty, she realized that with his family facing eviction, Michael would not leave for Liverpool, even if he somehow found the fare. He would have to stay and care for them as best he could.

What on earth was she going to do?

Suddenly, Edward Cavendish's face floated before her. With a sickening certainty, she knew that if she did not do something, she would be forced to marry him and Michael's family would be evicted; that, whatever she did, Michael's family would be evicted anyway.

All afternoon she thought, but no good ideas came into her mind. Panic-stricken, she found it difficult to reason clearly. For a long time, she gazed out of her window at the land that she loved; its gentle beauty gave her a little comfort. Finally, she gathered herself together, decided to try to talk to her father. If he did not insist upon her marrying Edward Cavendish, then at least one of her worries would be over – and she would have more time to do something to help Michael.

He looked at her coldly when she knocked at the door of his study and then asked him if she could talk to him.

"I don't have much time, Elizabeth. I'm very busy."

She took a breath. "Edward Cavendish asked me to marry him."

"So your mother told me."

Elizabeth gulped. "Father, I don't want to marry him."

Lord Roscawl frowned. "It's a bit late to change your mind. Your mother told me you had already accepted."

"Only because she forced me too."

"Elizabeth, really…"

"Do I have to marry him?" she blurted.

"Your mother's of the opinion, and I agree, that it's in your best interests if you settle down. She's planning to leave for London soon. If you back down on your promise to marry the young Cavendish, then you'll cause us all a great deal of embarrassment. Then again, you seem to enjoy causing us embarrassment. Don't you?" He waited for her reply.

"No, I don't," she said, stiffly. She could tell by his attitude that he had little or no sympathy for her.

"The young Cavendish is a good match, a far better match than you've a right to expect. Of course, I cannot force you to marry him, but, if you've any sense, you will. Your mother and I both feel that it is the right thing to do. Any sensible girl would listen to the advice of her parents."

"Yes, Father," she said, meekly.

It did not matter, she thought. Whatever happened, whatever her parents did, she would never marry Edward Cavendish. Though she had expected her father's disinterest, it hurt to know that he did not care for her feelings.

The plan came to her that night, as she lay awake watching the passage of the moon over the velvety black Irish sky. It was not perfect, and it was risky but, with luck, it would work. The more she thought about it, the more she became sure that it would work. It had to; she had no other choice.

In the morning, she waited until her brothers had gone out for a ride and her father was working in his study, then she walked along to the gunroom at the end of the corridor. She had only been in the room once or twice before; she did not like guns, hated the sound that they made. The racks of rifles and muskets made her shiver. In a drawer, she found what she was looking for, a pair of percussion pistols made by Staudenmeyer of London.

One day a couple of years ago, before he had gone to Oxford, Albert had taken these pistols out to practise shooting pigeons. Although Elizabeth hated the idea of killing anything, she had been curious to know how the guns worked and Albert had shown her. The mechanism was simple, she had just to put a pellet in the chamber and load a percussion cap and then it was ready to fire.

The gun was heavy, it was difficult to hold it straight, but she had some time to practise. She took both pistols, a handful of pellets and two packets of percussion caps, which she bundled into a pillow case and carried upstairs to her bedroom, where she hid them in the bottom of her chest.

The next part of her plan was easier. Elizabeth went to the storeroom beyond the bedrooms where her brothers' old clothes were kept, and found a pair of trousers, a shirt and a jacket that fitted her. In the cloakroom downstairs she found an old cap that her father sometimes wore when he went stalking; he would not miss it. Back in her bedroom, she tried the clothes on and looked at her reflection in the mirror. From a distance, she thought, she could pass as a man. She would have to cover her face with a scarf.

She spent the rest of the day practising holding the pistol. By dinnertime, she could hold it in one hand without it wavering.

It would do, she thought. She had no intention of firing it.

Eithne brought her tea on Sunday morning. Elizabeth looked at the maid, puzzled. Usually, she went to early mass and one of the kitchen maids brought her tea. The maid smiled at her then opened her wardrobe and began to take clothes out.

"Aren't you going to church?" Elizabeth asked her.

"I doubt I'll have time," Eithne replied. "The Lord will have to forgive me missing it for once."

"Why not?"

Eithne turned to her. "Didn't your mother tell you?"

"Tell me what?"

"You're going to London tomorrow. I've got to get you all packed and ready."

Elizabeth sat up in bed, shocked. Her mother had said nothing to her; in fact, she had not seen her since the shoot because she'd been in bed.

"I thought she wasn't well," she said.

"She must be feeling better. She told Brigid last night. I thought you knew all about it."

Elizabeth got up and dressed quickly, wondering what on earth to do. She had thought she had a week or more to put her plan into action; she had no idea that her mother was intending to leave so soon.

After breakfast, she went with her brothers and father to the service in the Church of Ireland chapel in the castle grounds. It was the only time in the week that she was allowed to go out of doors, and usually she relished the short walk for the brief breath of fresh air, but today she hardly noticed it.

The sermon was short; her father disliked long theological monologues and the minister who came from Kilkenny knew that. Elizabeth did not notice that the service was over until her father rose to leave; she was too busy thinking.

Back at the castle, Eithne was nearly finished packing.

"I'm not feeling very well," Elizabeth said. "I think I'll lie down for a bit."

The maid looked concerned. "Are you sickening for something, Miss Elizabeth?"

"No, Eithne. It's just that time of the month, you know." It was not, but the maid accepted the lie.

"I'll just warm the bed for you, Miss Elizabeth."

The maid's concern made her feel guilty. "No," she said, "don't bother. I'll be fine once I've had a nap."

"Shall I wake you for dinner?"

"No. I haven't been sleeping well, I'm very tired. I'll ring if I need you."

The maid smiled and left. Elizabeth listened to her fading footsteps, then murmured a brief prayer. There was no choice; if she wanted to run away, she had to go now.